"I want you to kiss me."

Stunned, shocked, Grady gaped. "You want what?"

She gave him a fleeting smile. "I guess that's my answer, huh?" She turned toward the door.

"Rachel, wait." He lunged to his feet and reached for her. His knee gave again, and again she caught him.

But he caught her, too. Caught her, wrapped his arms around her and held her close. Maybe, he thought, if he kissed her, he could get her out of his head once and for all. The reality of kissing Rachel could be nearly as staggering as his memories.

An instant later, when his mouth settled on hers, he knew he'd been wrong. On both counts. Kissing Rachel was even more staggering than he'd remembered. And it wasn't about to get her out of his head.

Not now, not ever…

* * * * *

Don't miss the next installment of
the Wilders of Wyatt County, where their hearts are
as big as the wide open Wyoming sky!

Dear Reader,

Welcome to a spectacular month of great romances as we continue to celebrate Silhouette's 20th Anniversary all year long!

Beloved bestselling author Nora Roberts returns with *Irish Rebel*, a passionate sequel to her very first book, *Irish Thoroughbred*. Revisit the spirited Grant family as tempers flare, sparks fly and love ignites between the newest generation of Irish rebels!

Also featured this month is Christine Flynn's poignant THAT'S MY BABY! story, *The Baby Quilt*, in which a disillusioned, high-powered attorney finds love and meaning in the arms of an innocent young mother.

Silhouette reader favorite Joan Elliott Pickart delights us with her secret baby story, *To a MacAllister Born*, adding to her heartwarming cross-line miniseries, THE BABY BET. And acclaimed author Ginna Gray delivers the first compelling story in her series, A FAMILY BOND, with *A Man Apart*, in which a wounded loner lawman is healed heart, body and soul by the nurturing touch of a beautiful, compassionate woman.

Rounding off the month are two more exciting ongoing miniseries. From longtime author Susan Mallery, we have a sizzling marriage-of-convenience story, *The Sheik's Secret Bride*, the third book in her DESERT ROGUES series. And Janis Reams Hudson once again shows her flair for Western themes and Native American heroes with *The Price of Honor*, a part of her miniseries, WILDERS OF WYATT COUNTY.

It's a terrific month of page-turning reading from Special Edition. Enjoy!

All the best,

Karen Taylor Richman
Senior Editor

Please address questions and book requests to:
Silhouette Reader Service
U.S.: 3010 Walden Ave., P.O. Box 1325, Buffalo, NY 14269
Canadian: P.O. Box 609, Fort Erie, Ont. L2A 5X3

JANIS REAMS HUDSON

THE PRICE OF HONOR

Silhouette®

SPECIAL EDITION®

Published by Silhouette Books
America's Publisher of Contemporary Romance

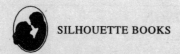

SILHOUETTE BOOKS

ISBN 0-373-24332-4

THE PRICE OF HONOR

Copyright © 2000 by Janis Reams Hudson

This edition published by arrangement with Harlequin Books S.A.

Visit Silhouette at www.eHarlequin.com

Printed in U.S.A.

Books by Janis Reams Hudson

Silhouette Special Edition

Resist Me if You Can #1037
The Mother of His Son #1095
His Daughter's Laughter #1105
Until You #1210
Their Other Mother #1267
The Price of Honor #1332

*Wilders of Wyatt County

JANIS REAMS HUDSON

was born in California, grew up in Colorado, lived in Texas for a few years and now calls central Oklahoma home. She is the author of more than twenty-five novels, both contemporary and historical romances. Her books have appeared on the Waldenbooks, B. Dalton and Bookrack bestseller lists and earned numerous awards, including the National Readers' Choice Award and Reviewer's Choice Awards from *Romantic Times Magazine*. She is a three-time finalist for the coveted RITA Award from Romance Writers of America and is a past president of RWA.

IT'S OUR 20ᵗʰ ANNIVERSARY!
We'll be celebrating all year,
Continuing with these fabulous titles,
On sale in June 2000.

Romance

#1450 Cinderella's Midnight Kiss
Dixie Browning

#1451 Promoted—To Wife!
Raye Morgan

AN OLDER MAN
#1452 Professor and the Nanny
Phyllis Halldorson

The Circle K Sisters
#1453 Never Let You Go
Judy Christenberry

The WEDDING AUCTION
#1454 Contractually His
Myrna Mackenzie

#1455 Just the Husband She Chose
Karen Rose Smith

Desire

MAN OF THE MONTH
#1297 Tough To Tame
Jackie Merritt

#1298 The Rancher and the Nanny
Caroline Cross

MATCHED IN MONTANA
#1299 The Cowboy Meets His Match
Meagan McKinney

#1300 Cheyenne Dad
Sheri WhiteFeather

the Baby Bank
#1301 The Baby Gift
Susan Crosby

#1302 The Determined Groom
Kate Little

Intimate Moments

#1009 The Wildes of Wyoming—Ace
Ruth Langan

#1010 The Best Man
Linda Turner

#1011 Beautiful Stranger
Ruth Wind

#1012 Her Secret Guardian
Sally Tyler Hayes

#1013 Undercover with the Enemy
Christine Michels

#1014 The Lawman's Last Stand
Vickie Taylor

Special Edition

#1327 The Baby Quilt
Christine Flynn

#1328 Irish Rebel
Nora Roberts

#1329 To a MacAllister Born
Joan Elliott Pickart

#1330 A Man Apart
Ginna Gray

#1331 The Sheik's Secret Bride
Susan Mallery

#1332 The Price of Honor
Janis Reams Hudson

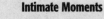

Chapter One

"Are you sure I can't convince you to stay for lunch?"

Rachel noted the sadness and exhaustion in Alma's eyes and smiled. "Okay," she said, relenting. She realized Alma didn't want to be alone while Joe was gone to the store. Alone, she would have too much time to think and worry. "Thanks. But I can't stay long." Her smile faded. "I don't need to be here when Grady arrives."

"Maybe not, honey." Alma placed a work-worn hand on Rachel's arm. "But you're going to have to see him sooner or later."

Rachel sighed and walked with Alma toward the kitchen. "I know. It'll be all right."

"Maybe better here and now than tomorrow during the funeral."

"Maybe," Rachel murmured. And maybe not.

And maybe she was making a bigger deal out of seeing Grady again than she needed to. Besides, he wasn't due for hours. Joe would be back from town soon. Rachel would be long gone by the time Grady showed up.

She was sitting across the kitchen table from Alma a few minutes later eating a roast-beef sandwich when they heard the front door slam shut and a voice call out.

Rachel stiffened. It had been five years, but she recognized that voice. It was *his*. Grady's.

It was too early! He wasn't due for hours. What was she going to do? How was she going to act? She wasn't ready to face him.

"In here," Alma called as she rose from the table.

Oh, damn, oh damn. Rachel could hear him coming down the hall to the kitchen.

Her reaction, she knew, was out of proportion. Ridiculous. Grady Lewis was nothing to her. He'd lost the right to be anything more than a bad memory when he betrayed her love and trust five years ago. She would be polite because he was Dr. Ray's son. Aside from her brothers, there was no man on earth she had ever respected more, including her own father, than Dr. Raymond Lewis. For him, she would face Grady and not allow the past to rear its ugly head.

Once Grady had been the center of her world, but now he would mean no more to her than a casual acquaintance. Someone she would nod to if she passed him on the street. Anything else would be inappropriate, considering the reason he'd come home after all this time.

But if he meant so little to her, why was her heart

pounding like the hooves of a hundred stampeding mustangs? Heaven help her, her mouth was dry, her palms were damp, and she hadn't even seen him yet.

Surprise, she assured herself. It was only the surprise of his early arrival. She hadn't expected to see him until tomorrow.

She placed the remains of her roast-beef sandwich carefully on the plate before her and pushed herself to her feet. "I'll be going," she said to Alma.

"You can't avoid him for long," Alma reminded her quietly.

Rachel forced a smile. "Of course not. But I'm sure the two of you have a lot to talk about."

Her smile faded. What they had to talk about was the fact that tomorrow they would see Grady's father and brother to their final resting places. That was the only reason Grady had come home after all these years. For the funeral.

Rachel turned toward the door, and there he stood. Grady Lewis had come home. The room suddenly seemed airless as he filled it with his presence. As she moved, she felt as though she were pushing through thick molasses.

He looked different, yet so much the same that it startled her. After the pain of his betrayal five years ago, anger had set in. She had fantasized that he'd gotten fat and bald and lost his two front teeth. Not very charitable of her, but then, she hadn't felt very charitable toward him in years. Hadn't felt anything about him. Not anything at all.

But her fantasies had been wrong. Devastatingly wrong. Grady Lewis was even more…impressive at twenty-six than he had been at twenty-one. His wide, Shoshone cheekbones were sharper, more chiseled, and he was bigger than she remembered. Not taller, but broader in the shoulders, thicker in the chest. He'd lost that lean, lanky look of youth and gained the solid build of a big, strong man.

His hair was shorter. He used to wear it halfway down his back. As a taunt, she'd always thought, a dare. Now that thick black silk barely reached his shoulders. But he was no less good-looking for it. On the contrary, he'd become a devastatingly handsome man.

His eyes hadn't changed. They were still the vibrant blue-green of a midday sea, and just as deep. The expression in them just as unfathomable.

Rachel took a small, calming breath. "Hello, Grady."

His gaze held hers for a long moment. Then he looked down at his side. "Cody, this is Miss Wilder."

Oh, God, oh, God, Rachel thought as she looked down at the little boy whose hand Grady held. She could hardly breathe. This was Grady's son. LaVerne's son.

The five-year-old boy held out his hand. "How do you do, Miss Wilder."

As far as Rachel could see, there was no resemblance at all to LaVerne Martin. But for his eyes— he'd gotten David's big brown eyes, Shoshone eyes, inherited from David and Grady's mother—Cody Lewis could have been cloned directly from Grady. He looked so much like that rowdy six-year-old she'd met on the playground her first day of school that it took her breath away.

Before Rachel could tumble back into those old memories, she shook the boy's hand. "It's nice to meet you, Cody.'' His hand was so small in hers, fragile yet sturdy. Trusting. ''I've heard a lot of good things about you.''

''From my grandad?'' he asked, his eyes wide.

Rachel squatted down to his eye level. ''That's right. And your Uncle David, and Alma and Joe.''

''Grandad and Uncle David died,'' the boy said matter-of-factly.

Rachel's heart clenched. ''I know, sweetheart. I'm so sorry.''

''They went to heaven to be with my mother and Grandma and Bozo.''

A lump rose in Rachel's throat. ''Bozo?''

''He was my puppy. He went to heaven last winter to be with Grandma 'cuz she was lonesome. But she's not lonesome anymore.''

''No,'' Rachel said softly. ''No, I'm sure she's not.''

''And Uncle David's all better now, too.''

While her heart broke, Rachel pressed her lips together to keep them from wobbling. She didn't dare look at Alma or Grady, or she would burst into tears. Meeting Cody's five-year-old eyes, eyes that were filled with wisdom far beyond his age, was difficult enough. ''Yes,'' she managed. ''Uncle David is all better now.''

Cody blinked up at her. ''Don't worry, Miss Wilder. It's sad, but it's okay to be sad.''

In that moment, it didn't seem to matter that this boy was the product of his father's betrayal. Grady and Rachel had been engaged to be married. They'd shared their dreams, their deepest secrets, their love, for years. And he had fathered a child on LaVerne

Martin. "Loose LaVerne," as she'd been known around town. And Cody was the result.

But none of that mattered as Rachel looked into those deep Shoshone eyes and realized she had just fallen in love.

She sniffed and offered him a smile. "You're a pretty smart kid, you know that?"

He smiled back. "I take after my dad." He looked up at Grady with all the love and hero worship in a young boy's heart.

Rachel looked around the room. Anywhere but at Grady or Alma. Anywhere to stem the flood of tears welling in her eyes. She spied her half-eaten lunch. Grabbing the plate, she whisked it away and threw the remains of her sandwich down the garbage disposal. With the manner of someone completely at ease in another's kitchen, she put her plate in the dishwasher and used the dishrag to give a swipe to the counter.

"I've got to be going. I'll let myself out."

"Are you going back to the clinic?" Alma asked.

"Yes." She grabbed her purse from the counter. "Take care. I'll…see you tomorrow."

To avoid having to pass near Grady, she left via the back door. *Escaped* was more like it, she thought with self-disgust. Why should she turn tail and run? She had nothing to run from. Just her biggest heartache. All six feet of him. And his son.

God, but it hurt to know that after one brief meeting, she was already in love with that five-year-old boy.

"Dad?"

Grady looked down and realized his grip was so

tight he was about to break Cody's fingers. He released the small hand instantly. "Sorry, pard. Did I hurt you?"

"Naw."

Sweet Lord, Grady thought. Rachel Wilder. She was still beautiful enough to steal his breath.

He'd known he would have to see her, because she worked at his father's clinic. But he hadn't expected her to be at the house when he arrived. Hadn't been prepared for that first sight of her.

He used to carry a picture of her in his wallet. Her high-school graduation photo. But he'd had to take it out when Cody got big enough to snoop and ask questions. Questions like, "Who's she? Why don't you have a picture of my mom?"

The photo had been several years old by then anyway, worn, faded and cracked. But his memories had seemed as fresh as yesterday, memories of Rachel on horseback, Rachel at the high-school football field, Rachel strolling beside him on campus at college. Rachel standing on her own staircase the morning after Cody's birth, tears streaming down her face while she refused to give him a chance to explain.

He had tried, really tried over the years to hate her for that. For her refusal to listen. Now and then he could actually accomplish it, but the hate never lasted for long. Even if she had listened to him that day, chances were that nothing would have changed. Things could have gotten even worse. As it was, he'd lost everything that ever meant anything to him, except Cody. But he could have lost Cody, too, if he hadn't taken him and left town.

He'd known Rachel would still be beautiful, and he'd been right. Just looking at her still took his breath away. From her shoulder-length hair as black as a raven to her smooth creamy skin and her Wilder blue eyes, she was nothing less than a knockout. Her reaction to Cody told him she still had that same inner beauty, too. A man would have to be a fool to walk away from a woman like her.

A fool, he thought, looking at Cody, or desperate. He guessed he'd been both.

He watched as Alma stared at the back door, where Rachel had just departed. There had always been a special bond between Rachel and Alma, and he could see that Alma was troubled.

"You're not going to hurt her again, are you?" Alma asked, still staring at the door.

Grady felt his shoulders slump. He'd thought... hoped for a different type of greeting from the woman who'd raised him. "Thanks," he said, bitterness creeping into his voice. "Yes, it *is* good to be home."

Alma pinched the bridge of her nose. "I'm sorry. That was uncalled for."

Grady wanted to shout, *Yes, it was.* He wanted this woman's approval, needed it. Desperately. He'd done what he had to do five years ago. He'd done the best he could at the time. He'd known then, as he knew now, that no one understood his reasons. But he didn't want Alma upset with him or worried about Rachel. Not now. Not with what they were facing tomorrow.

And really, what could he say to her about Rachel and all that had happened back then? He'd held the truth so tight for so long, had buried it so deeply, he wasn't sure he could bring it out into the light of day. Besides, Rachel wasn't the only one who had

had her heart ripped to shreds five years ago. She'd done her share of damage to him. By her refusal to listen, to let him explain, she had in essence made Grady's final decision for him.

Not that he had known what he would have said to her that day Cody was born and the whole town heard about it. All he'd managed to get out was "Let me explain."

Hell. He had no business dwelling on the past and thinking about Rachel instead of what lay before him.

"Forget it," he told Alma.

"You're right," she said tiredly. "Whatever's going to happen between you and Rachel is none of my business."

"Nothing's going to happen between me and Rachel."

"You're right again," Alma said, adding a nod this time for emphasis. "You've both moved on since then." She looked at him for a long moment, trying to smile but failing. Then she held out her arms. "Welcome home, boy."

"Damn," Grady whispered as he and Alma embraced.

Alma and Joe Helms had worked for the Lewis family since before Grady's first birthday. Grady's mother had hired Alma to help with the kids and the house. His father had hired Joe to run the ranch while Ray got his new veterinary clinic up and running. They'd been with the Lewis family ever since.

It was hard for a man to maintain his dignity when being hugged by the woman who'd changed his diapers and swatted his behind more times than anyone could count.

"I can't believe they're gone," Alma said, stepping back a minute later and swiping her eyes with the back of her hand.

"Neither can I," Grady admitted.

They stood for a minute, looking at each other, seeing the grief in each other's eyes for Ray and David and all that was lost. Then she hugged him tight again.

"Thank God," Alma murmured, enveloping Grady in her welcoming arms. "Thank God you're home." She squeezed hard, then thrust him back at arm's length. "Let me get a good look at you. Hmph. Good-looking as ever. And you brought that beautiful little..." She turned toward Cody still standing near the door. "Come here, you sweet thing, you."

Grady smiled while Alma nearly smothered Cody in hugs and kisses. Cody blushed, but to his credit he neither squirmed nor tried to wriggle away. Alma and Joe had come to see them last winter, so they weren't strangers to Cody. It did Grady's heart good to see him take to Alma so easily.

Since Grady's mother died before his fourth birthday, he'd grown up with Alma as his surrogate mother, his confessor, disciplinarian, coconspirator, knee-bandager, wound-kisser, advisor, and all-around best friend. There was no one in Cody's life to fill those roles but him, and Grady knew he couldn't begin to fill Alma's shoes, nor his father's, nor Joe's.

Finally Alma turned Cody loose and in less than two minutes had him seated at the table with a sandwich, a plate of cookies and a cold glass of milk.

Then she set a place for Grady. "You made better time than you thought you would."

Grady shrugged. "Couldn't sleep last night. Figured I might as well be driving. I called here and left a message on the machine, telling you I'd be early."

"I'm sorry. I've been ignoring the messages. Everyone wants to talk about the plane crash, and I just…"

"Yeah. I don't blame you," Grady said. He could barely admit to himself that his father and David were dead. He damn sure wouldn't want to talk about it to a bunch of people on the phone, no matter how well-meaning they might be.

A few minutes later, Grady had joined Cody at the table with a sandwich and a beer for himself when Joe came in with a bag of groceries. He set the bag on the counter with a thud. Grady had scarcely risen from his chair before Joe nearly hefted him off his feet in a bear hug.

"By God, boy, it's good to see you."

This man had played almost as big a role in Grady's life as Alma had. While Grady's dad had taught him how to ride and how to take care of a horse, it was Joe who taught him the finer points of horse training, how to rope a steer at an all-out gallop. How to fight, and how to hide the bruises from Dad. How to survive a hangover. How to hide a hangover from Dad. How to later confess to Dad about the fights, the hangovers, and anything else that needed confessing.

Joe Helms was a hell of a man. The only man alive good enough for Alma.

But it was Raymond Lewis who had taught Grady about life, about honor and integrity. That a man's word was more important than anything. How to be strong, and how to be gentle. How to love, how to laugh. How to stitch up a wound.

Suddenly the twenty-six-year-old man named Grady Lewis felt as small and vulnerable as a defenseless baby.

It was finally starting to sink in. His father and brother were dead.

Dad! David! What do I do without you?

Grady wasn't the only one feeling the pain of Ray and David Lewis's passing. As Rachel walked the two hundred yards from the Lewis home to the clinic, she struggled against tears.

Work. That was what she needed to keep the memories at bay.

But work would bring them, anyway. Just walking up to the clinic brought so many memories rushing back. Standing Elk Veterinary Clinic, the sign at the edge of the small gravel parking lot said. Raymond Lewis, D.V.M., Owner.

Rachel wondered how long it would be before Grady had the heart to take his father's name off that sign.

Grady's father, Dr. Raymond Lewis, was the first man outside her family that Rachel ever loved.

She smiled slightly at the memory. She had been five, and her father had been about to put her pony down because it was old and sick. But Rachel's brother, Jack, had defied King Wilder and sneaked into the house and called the vet. Dr. Lewis had arrived, and for the first time in her life, Rachel saw a man stand up to her father. It had been frightening, yet thrilling, because in doing so this stranger was saving her pony.

And save her pony he did. He gave it a shot of something—Rachel couldn't remember now what it had been—and the pony had recovered and carried her around the ranch for another two years, until she graduated to a full-sized horse of her own. Even after that, little Hopscotch was allowed to retire in ease; he'd lived another five years and hadn't been sick a day of that time.

Dr. Raymond Lewis had become Rachel's hero. From the first day she saw him, working over her pony, Rachel had worshiped the man. And she had known, right then, what she wanted to be when she grew up. She wanted to be a veterinarian. Even if she hadn't quite been able to wrap her tongue around the word yet.

Her friend, her hero. Her mentor. And now he was gone.

That fall, when Rachel went to school for the first time, she'd met the rest of the Lewis clan: Grady, an older man of six, whom she had fallen in love with and planned to marry until years later when he betrayed her; and David, age ten, who had grown into a beautiful man inside and out, with the eternal optimism and, sadly, due to a tragic accident, the mental capacity of an eight-year-old.

David, too, was lost to them now. He had died in the same plane crash that took Dr. Lewis three days ago. He would be mourned and buried alongside his father tomorrow.

Rachel shook her head and started around the building to the back door. The clinic was closed today, the front door locked. They'd given Jimmy, their part-time helper, the day off, but Louise was probably working at the front desk. Rachel would use the back door to hopefully avoid interrupting her.

It was incomprehensible to Rachel that a flock of geese could be responsible for the loss of two people so dear to her. Geese, of all things, flying a head-on collision course with the light plane Dr. Ray had been flying.

David had loved to fly. Dr. Ray had put off taking him up for months, waiting until Rachel finished school, received her veterinary license, and came to work with him at the clinic. Only then would he allow himself to take a day off and spend it with his eldest son.

Only when Rachel's lifelong dream of working side by side with her mentor was finally accomplished could Dr. Ray go out and get himself killed.

Damn! It wasn't fair.

Rachel jerked open the back door and barely refrained from slamming it shut behind her. Death wasn't fair. For that matter, neither was life.

And if she wasn't careful, she was going to start feeling sorry for herself, when nothing that had happened had happened to her.

Ah, yes. Poor me. I've lost my mentor and friend, and now I have to face the man who broke my heart.

Me, me, me. My, my, my. I.

What an ego she had. The world didn't revolve around her.

Rachel scolded herself for the self-pity. She needed to keep busy.

Inventory. That would occupy her mind. They would need an accurate inventory of everything in the clinic for the court once Ray's will was read.

Oh, God, Ray, I miss you and David so much.

Was it self-pity to wonder if she would still have a job after ownership of the clinic passed to Grady? As Ray's heir, he would have the final say over everything to do with Standing Elk—the ranch and the clinic.

One by one, every dream she'd had was crumbling beneath her feet.

Behind her the door to the surgery opened.

"Oh, you're back," Louise said. "I wasn't expecting you this soon."

Louise Hopkins was the clinic's office manager, bookkeeper, receptionist, and all around Jane-of-all-trades. Without her, Dr. Ray always said, there wouldn't be a Standing Elk Veterinary Clinic. The blue-haired grandmother of twelve had been working for him since his second month in business some twenty-odd years ago.

"How is Alma holding up?" Louise asked quietly.

"As well as can be expected," Rachel answered. "Grady's there now, and Joe just drove up, so she's not alone."

"Ah."

"What's that supposed to mean?" Whenever Louise said "Ah" like that, it was a given that she had just formed an opinion or was about to make an observation that a person probably didn't want to hear.

"Nothing." Louise waived a hand in the air.

Uh-oh. Denial. Another sure sign that Louise was about to trip somebody up.

"So tell me," Louise said with exaggerated casualness, "is he still as good-looking as ever?"

Rachel blinked once, slowly. "Joe? I've always thought he was handsome. He hasn't changed much since you saw him this morning."

"You're so funny. Of course I meant Grady. Not that Joe isn't handsome, I agree. But I'm used to his face. Seems to me Grady used to be one good-looking hunk."

"Why, Louise," Rachel said with her tongue planted firmly in her cheek. "Does Bill know you have these fantasies about younger men?" She wiggled her eyebrows up and down at the older woman. "Do your grandchildren know?"

Louise chuckled. "I'm not so old that I can't appreciate a prime specimen. And you didn't answer my question. Is he still a prime specimen?"

Rachel turned away, hopefully before the blush hit her cheeks. Prime specimen, and then some, she thought. But she wasn't about to admit she had even noticed. "You'll have to judge that for yourself. I'm going to inventory the surgical supplies."

"Well, you can if you want," Louise said on her way to the outer office. "But I did it yesterday."

Great, Rachel thought, her shoulders slumping. "Did you—"

"Yep," Louise called back from her desk. "Complete inventory. All done."

Hmph. "Okay. Great."

Rachel looked around at the immaculate room. Well, she could clean out the cages. But when she stepped into the kennel, the cages were spotless.

There were a thousand other things she could do. There was always work to be done around the clinic. But just then Rachel couldn't think of a single chore. Her mind kept straying back to the little boy standing at Grady's side. The boy with the big brown eyes.

Rachel understood the fundamentals of genetics. Dominant genes and all of that. Strictly speaking,

Both of the Lewis sons should have had the thick black hair, deep brown eyes, and dark-toned skin of their mother, Mary Standing Elk Lewis. The black, the brown, and the dark. Those were the dominant genes.

Grady and David had gotten Mary's black hair and coppery skin, but while David had those dark Shoshone eyes, Grady got Dr. Ray's blue-green eyes.

Now along came Cody, with all the Native American features from Mary, including the dark eyes.

He was a polite little thing, and so sweet it broke Rachel's heart. It appeared Grady had done a wonderful job raising the boy on his own.

"Busy," she said out loud. "I need to be busy."

In one of the recovery cages in the surgery room she found something that needed her attention. She had put a dog back together yesterday that had come out on the losing end of a bout with a barbed-wire fence. Now she could see that the poor canine had chewed the stitches open on his abdomen.

"Come on, fella, you can't get well that way."

Within a few minutes Rachel was busy applying new sutures and explaining to the sedated animal all the reasons why he should not eat this new set. She was certain he would be appreciative of her work, but doubted he would pay much attention to the lecture. She doubted, too, that he was going to like the collar she was going to put on him to keep him from reaching the sutures.

Cody had given up taking naps a long time ago, but traveling all day always left him groggy. Right now he was curled up asleep in Grady's old bed down the hall. The house was quiet. Tomorrow would be different, Grady knew. After the services people would come, bringing food for the survivors, and memories of the dearly departed.

He wished tomorrow was already over.

He wished he hadn't spent the last five years—Cody's entire life—living nine hundred miles from home.

For the millionth time, Grady wondered if he'd done the right thing in taking Cody and leaving town five years ago.

But dammit, what else could he have done, with the sheriff threatening to hand Cody over to the state to be put up for adoption? LaVerne's father, Sheriff Gene Martin, had a long arm and friends and family in every state and county office in Wyoming. Not to mention that the district judge was his cousin.

No, there had been no real choice. No matter how many times Grady went over it in his mind, taking Cody had been the only thing he could have done. He could not have stood back and let Cody be raised by strangers.

Of course, it might not have come to that if Rachel had let him explain. If she had only listened to him. Maybe someday...

No, there was no point. It was too late now. Five years too late for explanations.

But it was never too late for regrets.

Chapter Two

The funeral the next day was standing-room only, with more folks gathered outside the open doors of the church in hopes of hearing the service. Dr. Raymond Lewis had been one of Wyoming's most respected veterinarians, a long-time member of the Elks Lodge, and a good friend to nearly everyone he met. Farmers, ranchers, colleagues, and politicians from all over the state came to pay their final respects. Not to mention nearly every single soul in Wyatt County.

After the double funeral and graveside services, most of the out-of-towners headed for home, but the house at the Lewises' Standing Elk Ranch was nonetheless packed with people. They overflowed into the front yard and back, from the living room and den, and through the dining room and kitchen. Everyone had loved Dr. Ray, and those who weren't uneasy around the mentally handicapped had liked David. People shared stories and tales, laughter and tears.

But almost as prevalent as the topics of David and Dr. Ray in the dozens of conversations taking place at the Standing Elk Ranch that day was the subject of Grady Lewis's return.

Would he stay? Would he take off again?

And what, everyone wondered in hushed tones, was Rachel Wilder thinking about Grady's return? What was Sheriff Martin thinking about that little grandson of his—Grady's son?

Rachel heard the whispers, saw the looks cast at her, at Grady, at the sheriff. She couldn't do anything about Grady and the sheriff, but she didn't feel obliged to put up with the stares directed at her.

If pushing her way into the kitchen to slice sandwiches felt more like hiding than helping serve food, well, maybe it was. She needed something to do with her hands, a legitimate something upon which to focus her eyes while she tried to come up with a polite way to tell her lifelong friends and neighbors that her thoughts about Grady's return were none of their business.

Of course now that everyone was at the house, they could get a good look at Cody, if they didn't mind getting caught by everyone else staring out into the backyard at a bunch of little boys at play.

Cody hadn't been at the funeral or graveside. Donna, Rachel's brother Ace's housekeeper, had worked things out with Alma so that Donna stayed at the Lewis house rather than attending the services, and she brought Ace's three young sons with her. That way she would be on hand if people starting showing up at the house before Alma got home after the services.

Alma had apparently called Donna last night and asked if she would mind adding one more to the brood. Cody had stayed at the house with Jason, Clay, and Grant. Then others had heard that Donna was willing to watch their children, too, so they could attend the funeral. By now the eight or ten kids were probably fast friends. On her way through the house, Rachel had spotted them out in the backyard together while she tried to avoid Grady.

She hadn't been able to avoid him at the graveside services. Duty, and respect and love for David and Dr. Ray, dictated that she give the surviving family member her formal condolences at the end of the service. She'd done that, if a wobbly smile and a brief nod could be considered condolences. But that was all she'd been able to do without risking breaking down and crying at the thought of Ray and David's deaths.

She had cried plenty since the plane crash. Now she would think about something else.

But nothing else could work its way into her mind. Nothing but Grady. How long would he stay?

And why, she thought, angry with herself, was she concerned at all with what Grady would or would not do? She wasn't, she assured herself. Except for how his actions might affect her job and those she cared about, like Alma and Joe.

She wouldn't let herself worry about her job or Grady. This was a day to remember David and Dr. Ray, not old heartaches from the past or concerns for the future.

Ida Sumner worked her way through the gathering

of people blocking the door between the kitchen and the formal dining room, where most of the food was laid out.

"Heavens to Betsy," Ida cried, hugging a covered dish to her ample chest. "There must be a hundred people out there."

"At least," Alma said. "What have you got there, Ida? Wasn't there any more room on the dining table?"

"Truth to tell, I didn't even look," Ida confessed. She set her dish down on the counter. "This isn't for that crowd out there. I made it special, in case Grady came home. Told him over at the cemetery that I made it for him. Wanted to put it in here to be sure it didn't disappear before he had a chance to sample it."

Alma clucked her tongue and smiled at the same time. "I can guess without looking. Peach cobbler, right?"

Rachel smiled and ignored the pang of nostalgia that struck her. Grady had always had a weakness for peach cobbler, especially Mrs. Sumner's.

Ida laughed. "Right the first time. I didn't know what the little one would like, so I made chocolate-chip cookies for him. How are you doing, Rachel, honey?"

"I'm fine."

"We're all so proud of you for getting your vet license and all. A crying shame you didn't get to spend more time working with Ray. That man was a pure genius with animals, he was." Without giving Rachel a chance to respond, Mrs. Sumner turned back to Alma. "So what are you and Joe going to do? Do you think you'll stay on here at the ranch?"

Another pang struck Rachel. She'd been so wrapped up in grief over the accident that she hadn't thought about the fact that, depending on what happened to the ranch now, Alma and Joe might end up without their home, as well as their jobs. Surely not, though. Surely Dr. Ray had made some provision for them in his will.

Alma's smile was tight and tired. "I guess that depends on what Grady decides to do. He just got in yesterday. We haven't had the heart to ask him yet if he's made any decision about the ranch."

"Well, I guess we'll just have to wait and see, don't you suppose? Why, it wouldn't seem right, Standing Elk Ranch without a Lewis here. Without you and Joe."

Alma chuckled. "It wouldn't seem right to me, either."

"Ralph and I were talking just last night," Ida said, "about when Mary Standing Elk first came here and she and Ray got married. Oh, what a beautiful young woman she was."

"I wish I'd known her," Rachel murmured.

"You would have loved her," Alma said. "Everyone did. And she would have loved you. Lord, I remember the first time I saw her. Joe and I had just lost everything in a house fire up at Jackson. We were heading to Cheyenne to look for work when we stopped in Hope Springs. We had five dollars, a gasoline credit card, and not much more besides the clothes on our backs. It was raining, and there she was, walking up the highway, away from her stalled car, with five-year-old David by the hand, and Grady, just under a year old, in her other arm."

With a faraway look in her eyes, Alma smiled

fondly and shook her head at the memory. "We stopped to see if we could help. One look and I knew that David was special. I had a younger sister just like him—physically perfect but with a mind that would always remain childlike. I helped her with the boys, Joe worked on her car, and by that night Joe and I both had jobs here at the ranch. That was near twenty-six years ago." Alma smiled and shook her head again. "Never been anywhere else since. Never wanted to be."

While Ida and Alma talked about those earlier days, Rachel's mind filled with memories of its own about the Lewis family. Mary Standing Elk Lewis had died of breast cancer before Rachel knew her. Rachel's memories were of the Lewis men.

She'd met Grady on her first day of kindergarten, a couple of months after Dr. Ray had saved her pony.

Actually she met—or at least saw—David first, on the playground. He'd been ten, and some of the younger kids were picking on him, calling him ugly names like dummy and retard. Rachel hadn't known exactly what those things meant, but when she saw the tears well up in those beautiful dark eyes, she had wanted to cry with him.

She had yelled at the other kids and told them to leave him alone. No one had listened to her, of course. She'd been a tiny little thing, and not many outside of her own kindergarten class even knew who she was, much less cared.

Children, she thought now, could be the cruelest creatures on God's earth. The harder Rachel had tried to defend David, the worse the other kids became. They turned into a laughing, jeering, miniature mob.

Then, into the fray waded an older man—a first-grader with thick black hair and blue-green eyes. Except for the eyes, he looked a lot like the crying ten-year-old. But this boy wasn't crying, he was furious. Like a knight to the rescue, he pushed and shoved, shouted and punched, and taught those kids that if they made fun of his brother, they would pay the consequences.

His name was Grady Lewis, and Rachel had never been the same since that day. Sometimes she had thought of him as a hero, sometimes a troublemaker. But either way, she had thought of him, always. Throughout elementary school they snipped and sniped at each other one minute, then stood shoulder-to-shoulder to defend David the next.

Rachel smiled at the memories. She could do that now, smile at memories of her and Grady. At least those early memories. But it had taken her years to be able to do even that much after his betrayal.

There were more fights over the years for Grady. He refused to allow anyone to get away with hurting or making fun of David.

It wasn't until junior high that Rachel began to realize that she had a serious crush on Grady, and it wasn't until high school that he admitted he felt the same. From the time that she was fourteen and he fifteen, it was the two of them, always and forever. They knew each other's thoughts, shared each other's dreams. Grady, too, wanted to be a vet, like his father. Rachel and Grady planned to go to college together, then come home and join Dr. Ray at his veterinary clinic. Then...Rachel and Grady would marry and start a family.

It was seldom these days that Rachel allowed herself to remember that time, but today the memories seemed unstoppable. She and Grady had been so much in love, so close to each other, that when he graduated from high school he had stayed home a year and waited for her to graduate so they could go off to college together.

College had been exciting, hard work, and for a young man and woman in love, frustrating. But Rachel and Grady had agreed early in their relationship that if she were to get pregnant, her chances of becoming a doctor of veterinary medicine would be jeopardized, and neither of them wanted that. They were holding off getting married because Rachel's brother, Ace, had stipulated that if she got married before she was twenty-one, her college money would be cut off and she would have to pay her own way.

The memory brought with it a dull pain. Rachel often wondered if Ace had known something would happen to tear her and Grady apart the way it eventually did.

It happened the day they came home at the end of their second year of college. They'd arrived in Wyatt County late in the evening. Grady took Rachel home, to the Flying Ace. When he kissed her good-night that night, she'd had no way of knowing that within a matter of hours, her entire world would come crashing down around her head.

The next morning Laura Jane Brubaker had called to tell her that LaVerne Martin, the county sheriff's eighteen-year-old daughter, had died at the hospital the night before while Laura Jane, a nurse a couple of years older than Rachel, had been working the late shift. Rachel had been shocked, but wasn't sure why Laura Jane was calling to tell her this. Laura Jane was a friend, but not a close one, and LaVerne was no friend at all to Rachel.

Then Laura Jane had told her the rest. LaVerne had died after giving birth to the illegitimate son of the man who had brought her into the hospital late last night—Grady Lewis.

In shock, Rachel had hung up the phone and stared at the small pink roses on the wallpaper in her bedroom. She could still see those roses in her mind now. To this day she hated wallpaper with pink roses. She'd stripped it from her bedroom walls less than a week later because it reminded her of that phone call.

She had sat there that day, devastated by the news, and remembered the night the previous fall, the night before she and Grady had left to go back for their sophomore year at the university. They'd gone to a dance in town, and LaVerne had been all over Grady every time Rachel's back was turned. Grady had finally got so disgusted, and Rachel so angry, that they'd left the dance early. He had taken her home so they could get an early start the next day.

But he would have had to have driven back through town to get home that night. He must have seen LaVerne then. Must have…been with her after taking Rachel home. Because nine months later, LaVerne had given birth to Grady's son.

The realization had nearly killed Rachel that morning when she figured it all out after Laura Jane's call.

She'd seen Grady later that same day, when he had come to make excuses for what he'd done. To explain, he'd said.

To this day she had no idea what he might have told her, because she had refused to listen to him. To her way of thinking, there was no acceptable excuse for his having cheated on her, betrayed her trust, her love. God above, he had fathered a child on LaVerne Martin! *There was no excuse.*

She had refused to listen, had turned him away.

That was the last time she'd seen him, until yesterday.

Rachel shook her head at the old pain that threatened to rise. She had loved him with all her heart for years. She'd thought he had loved her.

She hadn't understood at first that he was gone, but it had taken little time to learn what had happened. When the truth came out, Rachel had been devastated all over again.

After Grady had left Rachel the night they came home from college, he had showed up at the hospital with LaVerne Martin, who had been bruised and bloody and in the final stages of labor. She had been living with her aunt in Casper for the past several months, so no one in town knew she was pregnant until then.

LaVerne died that night giving birth to Grady's son. The shock of the news had reverberated throughout the county. As had the story of how the distraught sheriff blamed Grady for LaVerne's death and had threatened to kill him. He'd also threatened to turn the baby over to the state adoption agency.

Before he'd been able to do that, Grady had taken the baby and fled.

Now, five years later, he was back, and people were wondering what Rachel was going to do.

She was going to do absolutely nothing. Grady's return had nothing to do with her personally. Whether he stayed or left had nothing to do with her, except as to how it might affect her working at the clinic. He had lied to her, cheated on her, betrayed her. Left her. Grady Lewis meant nothing to her. She refused to give him or his actions any control over her.

But he might have control over your job.

Damn. What a mess.

And what a coward she was being, hiding in the kitchen. From ghosts and rumors. No more, she decided, pushing away from the table.

Grady saw her the minute she stepped out of the kitchen. Like a pigeon coming home to roost, his gaze zeroed in on that cloud of black shoulder-length hair, that creamy, pale skin, those Wilder blue eyes. She'd grown even more beautiful in the years he'd been away. He'd known she would.

. The past tried to rise up in his mind, but he forced it down. It was a waste of time to remember. She wasn't his any longer. He'd given up all rights to her a long time ago.

If he stayed... Grady shook his head at himself. If he stayed in Wyatt County now that he was back, there was no way he could avoid her. She worked at the veterinary clinic right outside the front damn door. He was bound to run into her. Often.

God help him, he wanted to run into her, even knowing he shouldn't. She was still the only woman he'd ever loved.

"Grady."

The man holding out his hand for a shake was familiar, but it took Grady a minute to place him. Mack Norton. Owner of Wyatt County Feed and Seed.

"Mr. Norton." Grady shook the man's hand.

"I just wanted to tell you how sorry I am about your daddy and brother."

"Thank you."

"I don't know if you knew it or not, but David had been working for me for the past couple of years."

"He told me." Grady smiled. "In fact, he told me every time we spoke. He was proud as a peacock over that job. I can't tell you how much I appreciate your taking him on."

"Don't thank me. We were glad to have him. I don't know if you'll believe this or not, but he was the best damn employee I ever had. Never missed a day of work, unless the bad roads kept your dad from driving him in to town. And he never complained about hard work. Loved talking to the customers. Lord, how that boy could talk. And smile. Never saw him but what he wasn't smiling, no matter what. Sure gonna miss him."

"You didn't have any trouble from your customers about him?" Grady didn't have to explain his question. There were always people who felt bound to make fun of the mentally handicapped, or complain about them, or refuse to get near them.

"Oh, we had the odd incident now and then," Norton confessed, "but nothing serious. And usually nothing David understood. Except that one time when some newcomer stopped in and said something he shouldn't have." Norton chuckled. "He called David a dummy, and David fired back, 'Takes one to know one,' and stuck out his tongue."

Grady smiled at David's response, but he hurt inside that his brother had needed to defend himself.

Defending David had been Grady's job since he'd been old enough to understand that people could be mean.

Norton laughed again. "That guy didn't come back for about three months, but when he did, he apologized to David, and the two of them got thicker than thieves, they did."

Grady shook Norton's hand again. "Thank you. Thank you for telling me this. Thanks for being David's friend."

"Like I said, don't thank me. I might have been a friend to him, but he was a friend to me, too."

Then Norton was gone and Ida Sumner was there, bringing with her a flood of memories. Outside of his mother and Alma, Ida Sumner was the first woman Grady had ever loved. She must be near seventy by now. She'd had gray hair as long as he could remember.

When a young boy moseyed into Sumner's Drug Store with its exotic smells and old-fashioned soda fountain on a hot summer afternoon with nothing but lint in his pockets, Ida could always find a chore or two that needed doing and that paid just enough to buy a Popsicle. And later, when he'd outgrown the daily need for a Popsicle, she'd hooked him on her homemade peach cobbler.

"Boy." She'd always called him Boy. "It's sure good to see you. I told Ralph you'd be coming home for your Daddy and David, I surely did, never mind what anyone else had to say on the subject." The last was accompanied by a glare toward the sheriff, who stood with a group of men across the room.

"I was so positive you'd come," she said with a nod. "I made a peach cobbler up special just for

you.'' Then she leaned close and lowered her voice.
''I already took it into the kitchen. Alma's keeping
it safe for you. And don't you say I shouldn't have
gone to the trouble,'' she went on in a more normal
voice before Grady could say anything.

Not that Grady would have tried. No one ever got
a word in when Ida Sumner was talking.

''Your daddy was a friend to everyone in this
county,'' she said firmly. ''And David was a precious
soul. I've watched you boys grow up right before my
eyes, and if that doesn't make you part mine, then I
don't know what's what.''

''Thank you,'' Grady finally murmured when she
stretched up to plant a kiss on his cheek.

When Ida moved away to talk to someone else,
Grady turned away from the room and stared out the
patio door into the backyard. The cottonwood in the
far corner had grown some. Beneath it about a dozen
kids, Cody included, took turns on the old tire swing.
God, the memories that old tree must have. It was a
miracle it had survived all these years, considering
the abuse it had suffered at the hands of two growing
boys, not to mention their various dogs.

It struck him odd that there was no dog out there
now, yapping and leaping at the boys, running circles
around them or hiding under a bush while hoping for
a minute's rest from being pressed into service for
steer-roping or bronc-riding—the poor dog serving
as both steer and bronc, depending on a boy's whim.
There had always been a dog in that yard. David had
been crazy about dogs and couldn't stand to be without one. The last one Grady recalled was Harry.
Grady and his dad had picked him out together from
a litter of pups in town the last Christmas Grady had

been home. Harry was all black except for one white ear. He'd gone everywhere with David—including to California every time David had come to visit Grady. The dog had even gone flying with David and Ray. He'd been in the plane with them when it crashed.

"No way, man," someone whose voice Grady didn't recognize said from behind him. "No way will Rachel have anything to do with him again. She's too smart for that."

"Yeah, well, lock up your daughters and sisters, boys."

That voice Grady recognized, and the sound of it made tension coil in the pit of his stomach. It was a voice he'd hoped never to hear again for the rest of his life. Sheriff Gene Martin. LaVerne's father. Cody's grandfather, whom the boy had never met.

"I'd hate to see some other young girl end up dead like my LaVerne did at his hands," Martin said with a snarl.

There were a lot of things Grady Lewis would take the credit or the blame for. Some things he was proud of, some he wasn't. But whether he stayed in Wyatt County or left, this was one thing he could not, would not let slide. He turned slowly toward the sheriff.

"You mean beaten to a bloody pulp by her own father?" he asked coolly.

Around them, all sound stopped cold.

Wyatt County Sheriff Gene Martin was a big man, six-four and beefy, weighing in at over two hundred and thirty pounds. Some was middle-age spread, but there was still plenty of muscle behind it to back up the badge on his chest. Those muscles bunched now, and his face turned red and mottled. "Why, you no-good—"

"Come on, Gene." Ralph Sumner tugged on the sheriff's arm. "Leave the boy be. He just buried his daddy and brother."

"Like I buried my little girl five years ago." With a snarl, Martin tore loose from Ralph's hold and glared at Grady. "You were smart to run off, boy. Smart to take that little bastard with you."

From out of nowhere, Rachel was there. "Sheriff!"

"You'd do well to take him and hightail it out of here again the same way," Martin went on.

"Gene," Joe Helms said, his voice low and hard. "This isn't the time or the place."

"There's never a time or place," Rachel said hotly, "for a man to call his own *grandson* such an ugly name."

Shocked that Rachel would rush to Cody's defense, Grady deliberately kept his hands loose at his sides. If he allowed himself to bunch them into fists, he knew he'd be landing a punch in that fat mouth of Martin's without thinking. There was a time when he would have done just that, but he was older now, hopefully wiser. And if and when he ever figured out how to tell Cody that this man was his grandfather, he didn't want to have to confess to having come to blows with him.

"You've had your say," he told Martin quietly. "The last I knew, this house was still Lewis property. You've just worn out your welcome, Sheriff."

Ralph Sumner, Joe, and three other men crowded around the sheriff and herded him toward the front door.

Grady turned away, and there stood Rachel, staring at him, anger still flashing in her eyes. Again it struck him hard that she had taken up for LaVerne's son. She hadn't done herself any favors in Martin's eyes.

"You should have stayed out of it, Rachel."

Shock darkened her eyes. And dismay. She gave him a sad parody of a smile. "You're welcome, Grady. Think nothing of it."

Ah, hell. He'd said the wrong thing, hurt her feelings. *Good going, pal.*

He watched her walk away and lose herself in the throng of people. He turned back and stared out the patio door again. What difference did it make if she hated him even more now? What difference did any of it make now?

His father was dead. David was dead.

It was just like it had been for the past five years. Just him and Cody. They didn't need anybody else. They would manage just fine.

Yeah, right. Neither one of you needs a damn thing.

After the sheriff left, others began leaving. Grady wasn't up to accepting more condolences as they departed. He stepped outside onto the patio. The crowd in the yard had dwindled, too. It was down to four little boys now, including Cody. He watched them play, intent on letting his mind drift. A moment later the patio door slid open and a woman joined him. He'd seen her at the church, and again at the cemetery. Ace Wilder's wife, according to Alma.

"I'm sorry for disturbing you," she told him. "I

just came out to collect the boys. I'm Belinda Wilder.''

Grady said his how-do-you-dos and shook her hand, all the while waiting for the cold blast of disdain he fully expected from anyone in the Wilder family for what he'd done to Rachel.

''You're looking at me like you're waiting for me to bite,'' she noted.

Grady shrugged. ''I figure it's a distinct possibility from anyone named Wilder. Assuming they've filled you in on me.''

''They filled me in,'' Belinda told him easily. ''But I prefer to make my own judgments.'' She eyed him a minute, then frowned.

''You've made your judgement?'' he asked tiredly.

''No, it's not that.'' She shook her. ''Sorry. It's just that I feel like I've seen you before.''

Grady gave her a lopsided, wry smile. ''Maybe in the center of an old dart board or two out at the Flying Ace.''

Belinda laughed. ''It's not that bad, surely. No, I get the feeling I've run into you someplace, fairly recently. Have you been in Denver lately?''

''No.'' Well, that wasn't exactly true. He'd changed planes there a few weeks ago, but the only part of the city he'd seen had been the airport.

''Oh, well. It must be my imagination.'' Saying no more on the subject, she turned toward the backyard and let out a shrill whistle. ''Come on, boys,'' she called to the gang beneath the old cottonwood. ''Time to go.''

Four sweaty little boys—Cody and three blue-eyed, black-haired clones of Rachel's oldest brother,

Ace Wilder, tumbled up the yard and stopped just short of the patio. Dirt and grass stains covered their jeans and T-shirts, and all four boys looked as happy as ticks on a hound.

"Do we *have* to go, Mom?" the oldest asked.

"Yes, we *have* to go. Scooter's home waiting for you to feed him, and you've got other chores to do."

One of the boys nudged Cody and whispered loudly, "Is that him?"

Cody looked up at Grady with huge brown eyes and nodded.

Grady squatted down to the boys' eye level and bit back a curse as he felt his bad knee give a sharp protest. Damn the thing. It was taking forever to heal this time. If he wasn't careful he'd end up back in that godawful knee brace again. But for now, he would ignore the pain.

"Who might you guys be?" he asked, offering a smile that he hoped wasn't as stiff as he knew his knee was going to be.

"I'm Grant. I'm free," said the youngest, holding up three grubby fingers.

"No," Belinda said, shaking her head. "Grant Wilder is a clean little boy in clean clothes. I know, because I helped him dress this morning. You, young man, are as dirty as a little pig. All of you are. What did you do with my clean boys?"

"Aw, Mom." The oldest boy, about seven, wagged his head. "That's old. You told us to play outside. A guy can't be 'spected to stay clean if he's playin' outside."

"'Sides," said the middle Wilder, who looked to be about Cody's age. "There's no blood. You always say no blood is a good sign."

Grady glanced up at her. "I think he's got you."

"Hmm, yes, I do say that, it's true. Maybe you are who you say you are." Then she flopped her hands in the air in surrender. "I guess I can still recognize *them*, if not their clothes. The oldest is Jason, the middle one is Clay, and as you heard, this littlest piggy is Grant. Boys, this is Cody's father, Mr. Lewis."

"How do you do, sir," the three Wilder boys said in unison.

"Very nice," Belinda complimented. "Now say goodbye to Cody so we can go home."

"Sir?" the oldest asked. "Could Cody come out to our place and play sometime?"

"We'll see," Grady said. Not that he was sure he and Cody would be sticking around long enough for Cody to visit and make new friends. Grady hadn't had time to think that far ahead. Although it looked like Cody hadn't waited on him; he'd already made several friends. And these three were Wilders. How ironic was that? Their mother, no, stepmother—he remembered Ace's first wife, Cathy—might not have an opinion about him, but he wondered what Ace would think about his sons playing with Cody. Ace was as protective of the people he loved as a man could be, and he dearly loved his little sister.

"Okay," Belinda said. "Say goodbye, boys."

Grady bit back a chuckle at the various ways the boys dragged out their goodbyes to Cody, but finally Belinda herded her three into the house. Cody followed them to the front door.

Grady stepped back into the house in time to see Belinda and the boys stop and say goodbye to Rachel, then leave with the rest of the Wilders.

The Wilders weren't the only ones leaving. Nearly everyone else was heading out, too. Thank God.

Alma came to his side and patted his arm. "How are you holding up?"

"I'm all right. How about you?"

"Oh, you know me. Nothing keeps me down for long. We're sure going to miss David and your dad, but we'll make do the best we can without them. There you are, honey," she added as Cody made his way toward them. "Ida Sumner left some special treats for the two of you in the kitchen."

"Who's Ida Sum...Sum..."

"Sumner," Grady supplied. "She's a very nice lady who used to make the best peach cobbler this side of heaven."

"She still does," Alma told him as she led them into the kitchen. She dished up some of Ida's peach cobbler for Grady and a couple of chocolate-chip cookies for Cody.

The will was short and succinct, but it held a few surprises.

Cody was in the den watching a Disney movie on video, and three women from the church were cleaning up the kitchen. Everyone else was gone when the Lewis family attorney, Henry Baines, called Grady, Alma, and Joe into the room Ray Lewis had used for his home office.

The first surprise for Grady was that Rachel was also present. But then, he shouldn't have been surprised that his father had named her in his will, since Ray had always thought of her as the daughter he'd never had. Not to mention the daughter he'd once hoped she would become when she and Grady married.

Louise was there, too. Grady would have been surprised if she hadn't been.

David's will was simple, as he had owned practically nothing but his clothes. He had a small savings account of $5,000 from his job at the feed store. This he left to his nephew, Cody, to be held in trust for him by Cody's father, Grady Lewis, until Cody reached the age of sixteen, at which time Cody was to receive $3,000. He hoped the money would help Cody buy his first pickup. The rest of the money was to be held until Cody turned twenty-one.

Also left to Cody was David's dog, Harry. Of course, Harry had been killed in the plane crash, so it was a moot point.

David left his fishing tackle to his father, which meant it was now part of Ray Lewis's estate.

"It's legal?" Alma asked. "David's will? The court's not going to say that he was too incompetent or something, is it?"

Baines gave them all a reassuring look. "It's legal. David wasn't so incapacitated that he couldn't understand the meaning of what he was doing when he decided who he wanted to leave his possessions to. There should be no problem, unless someone decides to contest it."

The lawyer let them absorb that for a moment, then continued. "Ray's estate is a little more complicated than David's, but still, his bequests are to the point. You should know that he changed his will just a few weeks ago. Not because of any sense of impending disaster, but because his business situation had changed. Do you want me to read it, or just tell you?''

''Just tell us,'' Grady said, hoping to get this over with.

''Okay. Simple, then. Ray left ten thousand dollars to David, which now becomes part of David's estate, so it goes to Cody, to be held in trust until Cody turns twenty-one.''

Alma cried and Joe was left speechless when the attorney explained that their house—the foreman's house that Ray built for them years ago—and the eighty acres on which it sat, in the southwest corner of the Standing Elk Ranch, was to be deeded to them, lock, stock, and fencepost, along with five thousand dollars in cash.

To his grandson, Cody, Ray left his fishing tackle, the family photo albums, his University of Wyoming baseball cap, and ten thousand dollars, the latter to be held in trust by Grady until Cody's twenty-fifth birthday.

''To Louise Hopkins, without whom there might not be a Standing Elk Veterinary Clinic, or at least not one with the assets it now enjoys, I leave twenty percent of the clinic.''

The gasp that came as Louise sucked in a shocked breath was highly audible. ''Oh! Oh, my. Oh, Ray, you didn't.''

''Yes,'' the attorney said. ''He did. There are certain stipulations, which I'll get to in a minute, but he left you twenty percent of the business, with the understanding that the clinic does not own the land on which it sits.''

''Well, of course it doesn't,'' Louise said. ''I

ought to know, since I write out the lease check every month to Standing Elk Ranch.''

''Just so we're straight on that.''

''We're straight,'' Louise said. ''I just can't be-lieve…''

''He left another twenty percent to Rachel Wil-der.''

''He *what?*'' Rachel cried.

Henry Baines smiled. ''You heard me. Twenty percent of the clinic to you. You'll have the same stipulations that I haven't got to yet, but he said…'There can't be a veterinary clinic without a veterinarian, and the only one I want is Rachel. I know she'll do me proud.'''

Grady had to look away at the sight of tears in Rachel's eyes.

''To my youngest son, Grady,'' the attorney read, ''I leave Standing Elk Ranch and all its assets. I place no stipulations on this bequest, but it is my earnest hope that Grady will preserve the ranch intact and pass it on to Cody when the time comes. If he cannot bring himself to stay in Wyatt County and feels he must sell the ranch, I hope he will not sell it to a developer, and in any case, he must make provisions for the clinic to remain at its present location if the clinic owners wish to remain. I also leave to Grady the remaining sixty percent of Standing Elk Clinic.''

Grady sat back in his chair as the truth hit him. His dad had left him the ranch. It really wasn't a surprise; there was no one else to leave it to. But hearing the lawyer say it out loud made it real.

He had options now. He didn't have to work for someone else. The ranch was small compared to a place like the Flying Ace, but Standing Elk would keep him and Cody fed and clothed and then some.

Did he dare stay and make a go of it?

His first thought was, this would sure put the sheriff's nose out of joint. But Grady had grown up some in the past five years. If he stayed it would be because he wanted to, because it was best for Cody. He wasn't about to stay merely out of spite.

There would be others besides Martin who wouldn't be pleased to see Grady Lewis back in town. He had to assume that Rachel was one of them. And now they were partners in the clinic, and he owned the controlling share. How was that going to work?

But in truth, Grady didn't know if he had it in him to leave again. He had already crossed the biggest hurdle, that of showing up after all these years. Yet if he stayed, his father's absence, and David's, would be that much more real to him. He would be constantly faced with their loss. Back in California where he'd spent the past five years he would know they weren't home waiting for him, but he wouldn't be faced with daily reminders that they were gone from his life forever.

And if he stayed, Cody could be hurt badly by the sheriff. Grady wasn't afraid anymore of Martin trying to take Cody away. Especially not after that scene today in front of all those witnesses. But he would talk, and it would get ugly, and Cody was so young.

"Well?" Joe demanded. "You staying, or going?"

It was a good question. An important one. A legitimate one for his foreman—*his* foreman—to ask. And the man deserved an answer. They all did.

The decision should be an easy one. This was his home. It was Cody's legacy. Still, something held Grady back from making that final commitment. He hedged.

"I'm thinking seriously about staying," he said.

Grady couldn't help himself. He had to glance at Rachel to gauge her reaction.

As near as he could tell, she didn't have one. She kept her gaze squarely on the attorney.

"All right," Baines said. "Let's get to those stipulations about the clinic. If either Louise or Rachel decides to sell her share, she has to offer it first to Grady. If he declines, she must offer it to the other twenty-percent-holder. If that partner declines, she can seek another buyer, who must meet with the approval of both of the other partners."

Rachel smiled. "Why do I get the impression he didn't want any of us to sell?"

"Gee," Louise said with a chuckle. "Could it be because he gave any two of us the ability to deny the third one the right to sell to a buyer of her or his choosing?"

"There's more," Baines said cheerfully. "As long as Rachel chooses and is capable, she is to be the senior veterinarian at the clinic, and as long as she chooses and is capable, Louise is to manage the business affairs."

Louise looked at Grady, then winked at Rachel. "Do you suppose he didn't trust us? The way I see things, I'm in charge of the business, and Rachel's in charge of the patients. That leaves Grady." She tapped a long, manicured nail against her chin and ignored the fact that he hadn't said he was staying.

"I believe we'll put him in charge of heavy maintenance and taking out the trash."

Amid the laughter that followed, Henry Baines stacked up his papers and prepared to leave. It was seldom that the reading of a will managed to generate such genuine laughter. In fact, he didn't think it had ever happened at any readings he'd conducted.

Ray, he silently told his old friend, *things look pretty good. Your clinic's in good hands, and your boy is surely coming home. I can see the way this place pulls at him. He'll stay. Mark my words.*

Chapter Three

Rachel had known that Dr. Ray would leave the ranch to Grady, but it was a full day after the reading of the will and the reality of it was only now hitting her. It was one thing to see him again after all this time, to speculate on whether or not he might stay. It was another to realize that he now had a perfectly legitimate reason to stay. A concrete reason. A ranch to run. Majority ownership in the only veterinary clinic in the county. Since yesterday she had thought of little else but the possibility of his staying.

It was a good thing this was a slow day at the clinic.

Maybe she could get herself together before their first client came in. Maybe no one would notice her hands were shaking.

It was no concern of hers whether Grady Lewis stayed or left, she lectured herself sharply.

Of course, other people thought she had an opinion on the matter. Last night she'd gotten three phone calls from casual acquaintances wanting to know what she thought about Grady being back in town. What she thought about his son. It was humiliating to realize that everyone was once again talking about the way he'd cheated on her and left her.

Poor Rachel, they had said five years ago. Poor, poor Rachel.

She hated pity.

What she wanted, she realized, was for Grady to apologize for what he'd done. For him to grovel. Swear his undying love and beg her forgiveness. So she could shove it back in his face.

He would be on bended knee, of course. No, both knees. Hands held out, palms up.

Ruchel, you'll never know how sorry I am that I hurt you. If you can't find it in your heart to forgive me, I will find the highest cliff and throw myself off.

No, that wasn't quite right.

Rachel my love, I stayed away for as long as I could, but I had to see you again.

No, not that. Something more…

It was a mistake. Rachel, you have to believe me. I never betrayed you. I know Cody has my mother's eyes and my mouth. But if you'll just give me a chance, I can explain.

Hmmph. Better, but implausible. Still…on both knees, hands held out in supplication, his face lined with distress. And the entire town watching and listening.

I needed money, you see, to buy you a present. There was this sperm bank. How was I to know LaVerne would go there and get my sperm? There was a mix-up. Mine wasn't supposed to be sold. I never cheated on you, Rachel. I wouldn't. I couldn't. I loved you too much. I still do. Please, please take me back.

"Are you trying to make it levitate?"

At the sound of Louise's voice at her shoulder, Rachel was startled out of her daydream. Chagrined for letting such foolishness fill her head, she grimaced. "What?"

"You're staring at that scalpel so hard I thought maybe you were waiting for it to jump out of the autoclave by itself."

"Oh." She offered Louise a halfhearted smile. "I guess I was wool-gathering."

"Anything you want to talk about?"

"Oh, it's nothing important."

"Good. Then you can quit strangling that stethoscope."

"What?" Rachel looked down to find her fingers twisting the instrument tighter and tighter. "Oh." She stuffed the stethoscope into the pocket of her lab coat and turned toward the small animal cages lining the back wall.

"It's Grady, isn't it," Louise stated.

Rachel's stomach fluttered. "What makes you say that?"

"Because I know you."

That was the trouble, Rachel thought, with having a friend who knew her so well. A friend she was going to feel guilty lying to, but a woman had her pride, didn't she? "Well, this time you're wrong."

Louise's look was ripe with skepticism. "Uh-huh. If you say so."

"I do say so."

"Hmm." Louise looked at her watch. "What you need to be saying is goodbye. If you don't leave in the next ten minutes you'll be late."

"Late for what?"

"The Hendersons?"

Rachel blinked. "What about them?"

"Hel-lo-o." Louise tapped her knuckles against Rachel's forehead. "Anybody home in there?"

It took a minute, but finally Rachel remembered remnants of a conversation about the Hendersons' horses. Something about—

"You've got to pull a Coggins on a couple of their horses. Girl, where's your head? I told you about it first thing this morning."

Her head was where it had no business being, that's where it was, Rachel thought with disgust. "Right. Sorry."

Pulling a Coggins was a simple enough procedure, drawing blood and sending it to the lab. She'd done several in the few weeks she'd been out of school, and so far every one had come back negative. As she got in the clinic's SUV a few minutes later, she hoped this one would, too. She'd rather not have to deal with an incurable, highly contagious virus like equine infectious anemia, if it was all the same to the powers that be.

Two hours later Rachel pulled into town on her way back to the clinic and checked her gas gauge. Time to fill up.

It wasn't the blood tests, or even the visiting that had taken her two hours, it was the distance. Wyatt County was sparsely populated, with barely thirty-five hundred people. But shaped like a rough square measuring sixty miles by sixty miles it covered thirty-six thousand square miles. The Henderson place was almost as far from town as was the Flying Ace, where Rachel had grown up.

She pulled into the gas station and up to an empty pump and killed the engine. It wasn't until she unfastened her seat belt and reached for the door handle that she realized the man standing on the other side of the pump, filling his pickup with gas, was Grady.

It startled her to see him standing there in the middle of town, doing something as ordinary as pumping gasoline. Not particularly because she'd been fantasizing earlier about him begging her forgiveness on bended knee, but more because she wasn't used to seeing him at all. Wasn't used to even the possibility of running into him.

But while he wasn't looking—apparently he hadn't noticed her as she had pulled in from behind him—she took the opportunity to look. For some reason, she didn't seem to be able to look at him enough whenever she saw him. Why was he so damn good-looking? Good-looking enough to make her heart pound.

And wasn't that ridiculous, for her heart to pound at the sight of the man who'd done her wrong?

She had often wondered what would have happened if LaVerne Martin had lived. He would have married the girl. Surely, after her having borne his son, he would have married her. Despite the numerous fights he'd gotten into growing up, Grady had always had a strong sense of right and wrong—that was what had gotten him into the fights. And he'd always been honorable.

But if he was so honorable, Rachel wondered not

for the first time, why hadn't he already married LaVerne, long before the night Cody was born?

If he was so damned honorable, why did he have anything to do with LaVerne in the first place, damn his cheating hide?

Of course the answer to the former was that he probably hadn't known LaVerne was pregnant. Rachel had to believe that. Had he known, he would have married her, no matter what.

That was the reason Rachel and Grady had never made love. Well, technically they hadn't made love. They'd done everything *but* that final act. They used to joke that Rachel and he were probably the most experienced virgins around.

But they had refrained from that final act because neither wanted to take a chance on Rachel getting pregnant. That would have meant they would have to get married. They were going to get married anyway—there was no question about that. But getting married before they finished college would have meant they would have been on their own. Both Grady's father and Rachel's brothers would have cut off their college funds if they'd gotten married before getting their degrees.

One part of Rachel blamed herself for Grady's turning to LaVerne. If Rachel had given herself to him, maybe he wouldn't have felt the need to go to a girl everyone called Loose LaVerne.

But another part of Rachel scoffed. Other men resisted such temptations. Grady could have, too, if he'd wanted. If he'd truly been honorable. If he had really loved her.

God, but it hurt to remember. Sitting there watching the breeze play with the ends of his hair, seeing the flex of muscles across his shoulders, remembering the solid feel of him… The pain was as fresh, suddenly, as it had been five years ago. And it shouldn't be. She'd gotten over him, moved beyond all of that.

And she'd be damned if she would sit there a moment longer and run the risk of his turning around and catching her staring at him. Okay, gawking. Drooling. Like some teenager gaping at a rock star. She opened her door and climbed out just as Grady finished filling his tank.

As he turned to replace the nozzle, Rachel turned slightly away so as not to meet his gaze.

Coward, her mind screamed.

Okay, so she was a coward. Being around him was going to take a little getting used to.

With a squeal of tires and a throaty roar of the engine, a snazzy yellow sports car zipped into the station, and Mavis Martin popped out like a cork held under water and suddenly set free.

Rachel nearly groaned aloud. Mavis Martin could try the patience of a rock.

"Grady!" Mavis waved and started toward him in her leather miniskirt, which was the same glaring yellow as her car. Her hair, a cloud of vivid red, bounced around her shoulders with every click of her three-inch heels across the pavement.

Mavis would admit, after a few drinks, to being thirty. After a few more she'd cop to forty. Rumor had it she was closer to forty-five, but only her plastic surgeon knew for sure.

"Grady Lewis, there you are. I'll bet you don't remember me. I'm Mavis Martin, Sheriff Martin's cousin?" She said it like a question while she held out her hand and peered over his shoulder at Rachel. "Well, hello, Rachel. Or, Dr. Wilder, I should say." She tossed Rachel a breezy smile. "I sure never expected to see the two of you together again. Especially so fast."

Rachel gritted her teeth, not daring to look at Grady. "We're not together," she muttered.

"No?" Mavis's smile widened. "Well, then. Grady, I wanted to be sure you'd be home later this afternoon so I could stop by and talk to you about the ranch. And I do hope that cute little boy of yours will be there. I caught a glimpse of him at your house after the funeral yesterday. He's just the spittin' image of you." She peered over Grady's shoulder again. "Isn't he, Rachel?"

Grady nearly choked. No kin of Martin's had ever thought a Lewis offspring, with his Indian heritage, was anything but rotten to the core. Not since the day Sheriff Martin's wife ran off with that Cherokee from Oklahoma.

Grady didn't dare look at Rachel. He'd known she was there before she'd had her car in Park. What he hadn't known was how to act around her, what to say. He'd chosen to say nothing.

But damn, Mavis Martin had gall, to throw La-Verne's son up in Rachel's face that way. If Mavis wasn't a woman, he'd—

But Rachel, it seemed, had a cooler head than he did. When she replied, her voice was smooth, calm, and, if his memory served him correctly, deceptively pleasant.

"Oh, I agree," Rachel said. "The spitting image. Except for his eyes, of course."

"Mmm," Mavis murmured. "I'm sure I didn't get

quite that good a look at him to see what color his eyes were. I was just so grief-stricken that soon after the funeral, you know.''

''Mmm,'' was Rachel's reply.

''Now, Grady,'' Mavis said, suddenly all business. ''As I said, I wanted to talk to you about the ranch.''

Grady eyed the woman and scratched the side of his face. He could smell a rat as well as the next man. ''What about it?'' he asked cautiously.

''About listing it, of course. I'm in real estate, you know. Your father—I'm so sorry, Grady.'' She placed a hand on his arm. ''He was such a good man. And I, for one, was certainly not immune to his...manly charms.''

That choking feeling came over Grady again. His manly charms? Was Mavis talking about his *father?* She made him sound like some kind of ladies' man.

''I don't know how we'll go on without him,'' she continued. ''Just last week he spoke to me about selling the ranch.''

''He *what?*'' Grady demanded.

''About selling,'' she went on, undaunted. ''You know, Grady, it was more than he should have had to handle, what with the clinic keeping him so busy. And since I'm sure you won't be staying in town long, I thought...well, word is that the ranch belongs to you now. So I thought, even though I can no longer do business with Ray, that doesn't mean I can't do business with you. I can still sell the ranch for you, like I would have for Ray.''

Mavis's earlier comment about Cody hadn't gotten a rise out of Rachel, but this one did. ''Mavis Martin, that's just about the biggest pack of nonsense I've ever heard. Grady, don't believe a word she's saying."

Two things struck Grady just then. First, he was disconcerted that Rachel would do anything that could be perceived as helping him, knowing what she thought of him. Second, it didn't matter that he had yet to decide whether he would stay or go; he knew only that he wasn't about to sell the ranch. Anyone who thought his father would have sold it was out of his—or her—everlovin' mind.

"Raymond Lewis would never have sold that ranch and you know it," Rachel said heatedly to Mavis.

"A lot you know," Mavis countered. "We'd been dating for months. I was a great deal closer to him than you ever were."

His father had dated Mavis? Grady wasn't ready to hear about this.

"We were *real* close," Mavis taunted. "If you know what I mean."

No, sir, not ready at all.

Since it looked like the two women had forgotten Grady was even there, he tipped his hat, then stalked to the office to pay for his gas. When he came back out they were still at it, but starting to repeat themselves. Grady tipped his hat again. "Ladies."

Neither woman seemed to notice him.

There'd been a time when he might have stepped between them, seeing how heated the conversation was getting, and that conversation being about his own father and all. But hell, the whole county thought he was a coward anyway for letting Sheriff Martin run him out of town, so no one should be surprised that he decided against getting in the middle of what was rapidly turning into a catfight. He got into his pickup and headed home.

As he turned off the highway a few minutes later onto the gravel road that led to the house, he shook his head. He just couldn't picture his fifty-five-year-old father dating a black-rooted redhead with a fake Texas drawl who was fifteen to twenty years younger than he was. A woman with the personality of a snake disguised as a chipmunk. It didn't fit.

His father selling Standing Elk. Who did Mavis think she was kidding? He hadn't needed Rachel to tell him the woman was lying through her teeth. Raymond Lewis would have cut out his own eyes before selling the ranch that bore his wife's name. The ranch that was, or so he'd said for as long as Grady could remember, his sons' heritage.

And why, Grady kept asking himself, had Rachel bothered to intervene? By all rights she should have encouraged him to believe Mavis. Should have urged him to put the ranch up for sale and leave town just as fast as he'd arrived.

Maybe it was the clinic. Maybe she was worried about what would happen to it if a new owner took possession of the land on which it sat. It made sense that she wouldn't want to see the ranch sold. As long as Grady owned it, Standing Elk Veterinary Clinic was safe. That had to mean a great deal to her. She'd wanted to work there practically her entire life.

So had he, for that matter. They had planned to work there together, he and Rachel, with his father. That had been their dream. The dream that, for him, had turned to ashes.

Stop it. He had no right to think like that. No right to regret. He'd known exactly what he was giving

up when he left town that day. He'd done it with his
eyes open. And his heart bleeding.

All he had to do now was decide if he was staying…or going. But whether he stayed or left again,
the ranch would not be sold. Standing Elk Ranch was
Cody's heritage now. Nothing was going to interfere
with that.

But just so there wouldn't be any question, he left
a very plain message to that effect on the answering
machine at Martin Real Estate.

All the way back to the clinic, Rachel fumed. How
dare he? How dare Grady Lewis simply walk off like
that when she'd been trying to set the record straight
about his father and the ranch? How dare he treat her
as though she were a stranger, not once even looking
directly at her. Of all the nerve. If anyone should do
the ignoring around here, it was her.

She had half a mind to march up to his door and
tell him just what she thought. By damn, she did.

Half a mind. That was, she thought as she neared
the clinic, a little too close to the truth for comfort.
What else but having half her brain missing could
explain the way her pulse had raced at the mere sight
of him?

A conditioned reflex—that was all it was.

She'd loved Grady Lewis since she was five years
old. From the time she was fourteen he'd made her
pulse race. She just wasn't used to being near him
lately. If he stayed around, her reaction would level
out. She would be able to treat him as though he
were a stranger. Or, at best, a business acquaintance.

Maybe he'd had the right idea in ignoring her.

If he stayed, she would just have to get used to

handling it. And she *could* handle it. After all, she wasn't a starry-eyed teenager any longer, at the mercy of her hormones, with a crush on the high-school hunk. She was a responsible adult, a respected member of the community. A Doctor of Veterinary Medicine. She was beyond crushes. Grady was just another man. A near stranger who happened to be her business partner, through no choice of either of them. Nothing more.

She pulled into the clinic parking lot, but when she got out of the truck she turned toward the house two hundred yards away and started walking. She would be polite and to the point. She just wanted to make certain he understood that Mavis had been lying through her pretty capped teeth. Dr. Ray would never have considered selling the ranch. She wanted to get that idea out of Grady's head immediately.

She couldn't imagine what Dr. Ray would feel if he knew that his family's ranch, the place he'd lived his entire life, where all his wonderful memories lived, could end up in the hands of strangers. Strangers who might want to split it up into ranchettes for city-dwellers who wanted to experience life in the wild—for a couple of weeks a year.

She had a brief, devastating flash of that happening to the Flying Ace. No! The idea was not to be borne.

In a state of heightened anxiety that she was quite certain was an overreaction to the situation, she kept walking.

Maybe not such an overreaction, she thought a minute later. This was beginning to feel like a mistake. A big one. She should have just gone to the clinic and told Louise what Mavis had said. Louise could have set Grady straight.

But it was too late to turn back now. Grady had already spotted her. He was standing beside his pickup with the hood raised. With one hand braced on the fender, he watched her approach.

Rachel halted twenty feet away, suddenly unsure of herself and doubting her right to butt in.

Nonsense. Besides, it's too late now—you've already butted in. Just go talk to him. Don't make him think this is hard for you. That you're nervous.

After all, what did she have to be nervous about? She'd known him once, but they were essentially strangers now. She was doing this for Dr. Ray.

Taking a deep breath, she squared her shoulders and took the last few steps to the side of his pickup.

When Cody jumped out from behind Grady, Rachel nearly stumbled. Somehow she had forgotten to prepare herself for the sight of the boy who looked so much like his father. Her heart stuttered, then picked up a slow, steady beat.

"Hi, Miss Rachel," Cody said with a grin.

"Hi, yourself, Cody." How odd, Rachel thought, that it was easier to talk to him—the child whose very existence had meant the end of her world—than it was to his father. "How have you been?"

"I been fine."

"Cody," Grady said, stroking a hand over the boy's glossy black hair. "Go inside and tell Alma you earned yourself a cookie and a glass of milk."

Cody looked up at him and grinned. "Just one?"

"No." Grady pursed his lips. "You can have two glasses of milk if you want."

"Aw, Dad, I meant just one cookie."

"Well, if you only want one cookie, that's up to you. If it was me, I'd ask her for two."

"Yippee!" Cody leaped into the air, then raced off toward the house. "See ya later, Miss Rachel," he called back over his shoulder.

Rachel couldn't help but smile at their play and Cody's exuberance. "He's adorable, Grady." She met Grady's gaze and forced herself to add, "You must be very proud."

"Of him? I am."

"And of yourself for doing such a good job raising him."

"Thank you. But I somehow doubt you came over here to compliment me on my child-rearing abilities." His eyes narrowed.

If Rachel hadn't known better, she would have sworn he was on the verge of laughter.

"You and Mavis get everything worked out?" he asked.

"Very funny. I can't believe you just drove off like that, when your ranch was the topic of debate."

"My daddy always taught me never to get between two females, especially if they're fighting."

She didn't care for that smirk in his tone and on his face. No sir, she did not. "Your daddy taught you a few other things, too, that you chose to ignore, like honesty, integrity, fidelity."

"I wondered how long it would take you to bring that up," he said grimly.

Rachel squeezed her eyes shut and tilted her face to the sun. "I'm sorry. I didn't intend to."

"Didn't you?"

She shook her head. "There's no point." Opening her eyes, she looked at him solemnly. "It was a long time ago. I only came over to make sure you know that your dad had no intention of selling this ranch."

"I never thought he did."

"Oh." Feeling suddenly foolish, she flapped her hands against her thighs. "Oh. Well. I just wanted to make sure. That you didn't believe what Mavis was telling you."

"I didn't. I know—" He stopped, swallowed. "Knew him better than that."

"He considered Standing Elk to be Cody's heritage." *Shut up, Rachel. Just shut up and get out of here. You said what you came to say.*

"He told you that?" Grady asked, clearly surprised.

She nodded. "A couple of weeks ago. Your father and I were friends, Grady. Why wouldn't he tell me?"

Grady shook his head and looked down at the ground, then quickly looked back up at her. "I was under the impression that Cody and I were off-limits as a topic of conversation between the two of you. That you didn't want to hear anything about us."

Rachel felt a blush stain her cheeks. She felt as though she'd just been caught doing something shameful or embarrassing. And that was just plain nonsense. After what Grady had done to her, she'd had every right to refuse to listen to his father sing his praises.

"That's true," she told him with an edge to her voice. "After you left town, I didn't want to know anything about you. Not where you were or what you were doing, or who you were doing it with."

Grady's head jerked slightly, as if he'd just been slapped. Rachel wished she could take satisfaction in that. Lord knew he had it coming. But somehow the satisfaction she once thought she would feel at tossing his misdeeds back in his face simply wasn't there. She wasn't sure what that meant, but it left her feeling off-center, as if the ground were suddenly two inches lower than it had been.

"Your dad didn't mention you when he brought up the subject of the ranch," she said. "He was just talking about all the things that needed doing around the place and how he wanted to keep it in good shape to pass along to his grandson. He was not thinking of selling it."

"Okay."

She wasn't going to ask. She didn't want to know. It was none of her business. She opened her mouth to say goodbye. Instead, the question she wasn't going to ask came out. "Are you really going to stay?"

He stuffed his hands into the back pockets of his jeans and threw his weight onto one leg, taking on that cocky, sexy stance that used to send her teenage hormones into overdrive. How odd that it seemed to have the same effect on her now, when she wanted nothing to do with him.

"Never mind," she said in a rush. "It's none of my business. I just wanted you to know that Mavis was lying."

He narrowed one eye and looked at her oddly. "Was she lying about...dating him, too?"

Rachel held up both hands and took a step backward. "About that, I have no idea." She gave an exaggerated shudder. "I don't want to know. But surely he had better taste than that."

Grady almost laughed. She could see him choking it back.

"Well," she said, taking another step back. "I better get back to work." Then she added solemnly,

"I'm really sorry about David and your dad. We'll all miss them."

He gave her a nod. "Thanks."

There never had been much of a separation between employer and employee on Standing Elk Ranch, not when it came to the Lewises and the Helmses. For as far back as Grady could remember, Alma and Joe always ate with the family at what they called "the big house."

This evening was no different, but the group was much smaller than it used to be. Now there was only Grady, Cody, Alma and Joe. At least Alma had taken the center leaf out of the table so the absence of Ray and David wasn't so painfully obvious.

While passing the bowl of mashed potatoes to her husband, Alma looked across the table at Grady. "You're not really selling, are you?"

"The ranch?" Grady asked. "Oh. You mean Mavis. Word still travels at the speed of light around here, I see."

"Rachel told Louise and Louise told me that Mavis cornered you at the gas station. So, are you?"

"Selling the ranch? Of course not."

Some of the stiffness in Alma's shoulders seemed to relax. "You're staying, then?"

Grady couldn't count the times he had asked himself that same question. Particularly since the reading of the will yesterday, and after Rachel's visit a few hours ago. But when he thought of the ranch, he thought of Cody, of Alma and Joe and Louise. And Rachel.

No, don't think about Rachel.

But it was impossible not to think about her, about

the way the breeze had played with her hair, the way the sun made it shine. The way her jeans hugged her hips.

Oh, yeah, right. Like you'll ever get your hands on those hips again, buddy.

But a man could dream. And he had. For five long, lonely years. Futile, fruitless dreams of what once was, what might have been.

Dammit, he didn't want to want her. *Didn't* want her, and wouldn't. And he certainly wasn't going to let thoughts of her influence his decision whether or not to move home.

Home. That was the telling thought. He hadn't lived here in five years, yet he still thought of it as home. It still felt like home.

It was time to admit, Grady realized, that he'd been headed back, wanting to come home more than anything, since the day he left. But he had vowed to keep Cody as far away as he could from Wyatt County as long as Gene Martin still held a position of power there. The twenty-first century might be stretched out before them, but some aspects of Wyatt County still ran more like the nineteenth. The county sheriff could, if he was careful, get away with murder. Literally.

But Grady had made certain years ago that Martin would never be able—legally, at least—to carry out his threat of having his daughter's son put up for adoption. It was that threat, and the realization that the district judge was Martin's cousin and between the two of them they had the clout and the connections to pull it off, that had made Grady take Cody and run. Martin had said that as long as he never had to look at his daughter's illegitimate part-Indian offspring, he'd leave the Lewis family alone. Otherwise, there would be hell to pay.

Grady had looked into the man's eyes that night, less than an hour after LaVerne had died giving birth to Cody, and had known the man would do what he said. Nothing would stop him.

So Grady had taken Cody. He'd ended up about as far from Wyatt County as he could go without ending up in the ocean. Even then, it had been damn close. He'd ended up in Monterey, California, training horses on a top ranch.

He hadn't expected to be gone five years. A few months, he had figured. Enough time to make sure that his name as father on Cody's birth certificate was legal enough to prevent Martin from taking the baby. But it had taken time, and the longer it took, the easier it had become to stay away. Especially every time he remembered the disappointment in his father's eyes upon learning about the baby. And the pain in Rachel's. Both of them had refused to listen to him.

At least his dad had given him his car to drive when he left, instead of the old pickup Grady had driven home from college. The pickup never would have made it. The car had done just fine for three years before he traded it in on a newer pickup.

And now, after five years, he was back. Home.

He'd thought about staying. Last night he had pored over the ranch books to see what kind of shape things were in. While they wouldn't be able to live lavishly—they never had—the ranch would support him and Cody with no trouble.

All that remained was the final decision.

"Pard," he said, turning to Cody.

"Yeah, Dad?"

"What would you think if we went home, packed up our gear, and came back here."

"You mean to live?"

"That's what I mean."

Cody frowned. "Who would be our boss?"

"I would."

"You would? You would be our boss?"

"That's right. What do you think?"

"Who'd be my keeper?"

Joe chuckled at that.

"Well," Grady said, "we'd have to ask her, but my guess is it would be Alma."

Cody's eyes widened. "No foolin'? And could I go see Jason and Clay and Grant sometimes, and could they come see me, and could I have my own horse and maybe a dog, too?"

Joe clapped a hand to Grady's back. "Looks to me like you're staying, boy."

"Are we?" Cody wiggled out of his chair and jumped up and down. "Are we, Dad?"

Grady looked at Alma. "Are you up to the challenge of another generation of Lewis boys?" Grady asked.

Alma's eyes misted. "You mean it? You're moving home? For good?"

"If I can find the right person to look after my pard, here."

"You wanna be my keeper, Alma? Huh, do ya, do ya?"

"Oh, praise the Lord!" Alma cried. She rushed around the table and kissed Grady smack on the lips. "It's about time. Oh..." Tears welled in her eyes as she looked up toward the ceiling. Toward heaven.

"You hear that Mary? Ray? Your boys are coming home for good. I've got me another young Lewis rascal to take care of."

Grady felt his throat tighten. "Thank you, Alma."

She smiled, looked down at Cody, then back at him. "No, Grady, thank *you*."

Chapter Four

It wasn't the sight of Louise seated at her desk and laughing that surprised Rachel and halted her in her tracks the next morning when she arrived at the clinic. It was the sight of Grady sitting on the corner of the desk.

"Good morning," Louise said cheerfully. "Our new partner says he has something to tell us."

"Oh?" Rachel forced herself to move toward the cabinet behind the counter and put her purse away. She silently scolded herself for her rapid pulse and shaking hands, both of which had started the instant she saw him. It was just Grady. She'd seen him several times in the last few days. Her reaction was ridiculous, and it simply had to stop. Just as soon as she figured out how to control it.

The little lecture didn't help. As she turned back toward Louise and Grady she clasped her hands behind her back to hide their trembling and looked at Louise. "What is it?" she asked.

"I'm staying," Grady stated.

Rachel hadn't wanted to look directly at him if she could avoid it, but at his words, her gaze snapped to his.

"Isn't that wonderful?" Louise said.

Was it? What was Rachel supposed to say? Grady was staying. After five years, he was back, and he was staying. He would live right next door to the place where she spent her days. He owned the majority of the clinic. They were partners. Neighbors.

She'd known it was coming, hadn't she? How could he not stay?

It's nothing to you if he stays. He's nothing to you.

She was going to see him often, would constantly run into him, hear people talk about him.

"Nothing to say?" he asked her.

Not a thing, she thought, half frantic, half dazed. Or was it half angry, half—

No. She was not angry, nor was she glad. She wasn't even ambiguous, if that was possible. "Your dad would be glad." Oh, and wasn't that brilliant? "Alma and Joe must be thrilled."

Grady gave a slight shrug and looked away. "As far as the clinic goes, I doubt I'll ever have much to say about it. I'm not a vet, nor do I know much about running a business. The only thing I'll say is that you need to replace the receptionist who quit last month, and you need at least one other doctor here."

Rachel prickled up over that. "You think I can't handle it?"

"I'm sure you're a good vet. My dad wouldn't have had you here if you weren't. But he always said there was too much work in Wyatt County for one vet. He hired another one whenever he could get somebody to come here. Do you know of another doctor you could hire?''

Now she felt foolish to have thought he'd been criticizing her. "I can probably find someone."

"Good." He turned to Louise. "As for taking out the trash, you're on your own for the next week or so. We've got to go back to California and haul our belongings home."

"Cody's going with you?" Louise asked. "That's an awfully long trip for such a little thing, especially when he just made it last week."

"I know. I gave him his choice. He wants to pack his own things and say goodbye to his friends."

The phone on Louise's desk rang.

Grady stood and stepped away from the desk. "I'll let you two get to work."

"Drive safely," Louise told him.

While Louise took the call, Grady left, and Rachel went to the back room, out of Louise's line of vision.

He's staying.

The week following Grady's announcement was a hectic one for Rachel, proving Grady's point that the clinic needed another vet on staff. Between pets being brought into the clinic and calls on farms and ranches to work on cattle and horses, and even one annoying Don Juan of a goat named Harley, not to mention the record-keeping that all this work required, Rachel was run ragged. She didn't have much time to think about Grady moving home, and for that she was grateful.

The work was exhausting yet exhilarating. It was

her lifelong dream come true. If part of that dream was missing, at least she was still able to practice her chosen profession. She would forever miss Dr. Ray, but she liked to pretend that he was watching over her shoulder. She knew there would be many times she would wish he really was, so she could ask his advice and rely on his vast experience to help her help the animals in her care.

And if the other part of her dream had been to work side by side with Grady, well, she'd given up on that idea a long, long time ago. She hadn't allowed herself to dwell on it.

Nor would she dwell on it this day. It was Sunday, and she was headed home. Or rather, Home, with a capital H. That's how she thought of the Flying Ace, where she'd been born and raised.

Rachel didn't live on the Flying Ace any longer. Hadn't, really, since she'd started college seven years ago. Even most of her summers during college had been spent working in the school's veterinary lab where she could gain experience she knew would prove useful in her career. But when she'd received her veterinary license a few weeks ago and come home to Wyatt County for good, her brothers had surprised her—completely bowled her over—by presenting her with a house in town, barely four miles from Standing Elk Clinic, as her graduation present.

She'd been stunned by their generosity. Especially considering that they had just finished paying for seven years of her college expenses, insisting that she put her own portion of the Flying Ace income away in savings and let it build.

So now she had a nice nest egg—invested in mutual funds; no tame savings account for her—and a comfortable, pretty two-bedroom house in town. Plus she still had her share of the Flying Ace, she reminded herself as she turned off the highway onto the ranch road. She slowed her little red sports car, which she'd bought two weeks ago from Belinda. In theory, she slowed to take the cattle guard at a safe speed in the low-slung car. In fact, however, she slowed at the spot no matter what she was driving, because she always got a thrill out of looking up at the Flying Ace sign that arched over the road.

Lord, how she loved this ranch.

A rooster tail of dust sailed up in her wake as she gave the car its head and raced along the gravel road toward the house.

Rachel's parents, King and Betty Wilder, had died when Rachel was twelve. Her oldest brother, Ace, had been twenty at the time and had inherited sixty percent of the ranch, with the remaining forty percent divided equally among Jack, Trey, and Rachel.

Well, actually, King Wilder's will had not specifically named who got the other forty percent. He had stipulated that it was to be divided equally among all his "other children."

According to Jack, the old man had been hedging his bets. The rest of them had come to the same conclusion, but none of them would have said it for fear of offending Jack.

It was no secret that Jack, the second eldest Wilder offspring, was actually only a half brother to the other three. His mother had been a barmaid over in Cheyenne; his birth had been illegitimate. None of the family, including King, had known of Jack's existence until the boy's mother died and his aunt drove

up and dumped him, literally, on the doorst
Jack was twelve.

Rachel had barely been five when Jack came to
live with them, but she remembered the shock, her
mother's tears, her father's blustering pride at having
produced another son. He'd been tickled to death that
the boy had been named Jack. As far as King Wilder
was concerned, this Jack was a gift, meant to take
the place of the baby boy who'd died before reaching
his first birthday. That son, who would have been the
same age as this Jack, had also been named Jack.

It was a sign, King had said. This son was meant
to take his rightful place on the Flying Ace. King
had promptly had Jack's last name legally changed
to Wilder.

From there the deck of cards fanned out: King, the
father—or sire, as he'd liked to call himself—Ace,
Jack, Trey and Rachel.

It had been a major miracle that Rachel hadn't
ended up being named Queen, but her mother, God
bless her, had put her foot down at that, just as she'd
done when King wanted to name their youngest son
Ten. Betty, so the story went, had said, "And if we
have another, will he be Nine?" Still grieving over
the death of their infant son Jack, and still smarting
at learning that her husband had recently had an affair, she was in no mood, as Aunt Mary told the
story, to humor King.

They had compromised on Trey.

Rachel, too, had been a compromise. Or rather, her
name had. Most people didn't know that the face
cards of a deck of playing cards had names. The
Queen of Spades was Palas. That wouldn't do. Neither would Argine, the Queen of Clubs. King had

pushed for Judith because he liked the idea of his daughter—if he had to have a daughter—being named after the Queen of Hearts.

But Betty knew of three babies born in the county that very year who'd been named Judith, Jude, and Judy. She put her foot down again and held out for Rachel, the Queen of Diamonds.

She'd won.

Five years later, when King's illegitimate son arrived, Betty had been devastated. But she'd known about her husband's affair—she'd threatened to leave him at the time, but he swore it would never happen again. So she wasn't completely surprised by the existence of a child. Devastated, but not surprised.

As Rachel parked her car next to Belinda's new station wagon, she remembered the sadness that never left her mother's eyes after Jack came. It made her hurt for both of them, for none of what happened had been her mother's fault, or Jack's.

Not that Ace and Trey had been willing to give their new brother a break when he'd arrived. They took their cue from their mother. They didn't need or want another brother, and that was that. Until five-year-old Rachel had declared that Jack was just as much her brother as were Ace and Trey.

Oh, the power of a five-year-old girl in a house full of males, Rachel thought now as she looked around the yard at her family. Especially a little girl who was spoiled rotten by her parents and brothers. No one had dared upset her by picking on Jack after she'd staked her claim on him. And she'd never been sorry.

Three weeks later, when her father wanted to put down her pony, it was Jack who had defied him and called the vet. It was thanks to Jack that Rachel not only got to keep her precious pony, but that she met Dr. Ray, and found her mission in life.

God bless Jack Wilder.

Even Jack himself chuckled, albeit with sarcasm, at the wording of their father's will, when instead of naming his remaining three children, he'd written that the other forty percent of the Flying Ace was to be divided equally among his "other children."

For weeks after the reading of the will, they all walked around waiting for another of King Wilder's surprise offsprings to show up. No one would have been too shocked if one had.

But no one showed up to make such a claim, so they remained four. And here they were, cooking hamburgers on the grill in the yard on a Sunday afternoon, all four siblings, plus Ace's wife and three sons, along with Donna Harris, their housekeeper.

Stoney Hamilton was there, too. He'd been foreman of the Flying Ace for more years than Rachel had been alive. He'd stepped down several years ago and let Jack take over, but he still had contributions to make, work he wanted to do. He was still needed on the Flying Ace and would always have a place there.

Frank Thompson, Ace's top horse trainer, could rarely be dragged away from his horses. But for a family get-together, not to mention a bowl of Donna's banana pudding, he had not only left the stables, but had shined his boots.

"Yes, sir," he told Rachel, "it sure is great to have you back home for good, girl."

Frank was one of Rachel's favorite people. She gave him a hug. "It's good to finally be home," she told him. "Even if home is in town now instead of out here."

"No matter where you live, girl," Frank said, "the Flying Ace will always be your home."

"Aunt Rachel, Aunt Rachel!" Clay, her five-year-old nephew, raced up and tugged on her arm. "Aunt Rachel, Scooter gots a thorn in his paw. You gotta fix it. You gotta operate."

Frank winked at her. "Sounds like a job for Dr. Wilder."

"Who?" Clay wanted to know.

"Never mind." Rachel laughed and shook her head at Frank. To Clay she said, "Show me this alleged thorn."

"It's not a ledgend thorn." Clay took her by the hand and pulled her around to the side of the house where the boys were playing with their dog. "I think it's just a plain ol' thorn. You know, the kind that hurts? You might need your doctor bag."

"I might, huh?" Young Clay was fascinated with wounds of any type, be they on people or animals. Especially if they bled. Rachel figured he was going to grow up to be a trauma surgeon or a vampire, she wasn't sure which. "Well, let's have a look first."

She could tell at once how much so-called pain the dog was in. His tail was wagging so hard his entire body, about the size of a small sofa, was wagging with it, and his tongue lolled out in a happy doggy grin. He wanted to play so badly, it took all three boys to hold him still so Rachel could look at his paw. She was beginning to think she'd been had, and braced herself for the boys to launch themselves at her in a fit of giggles, but eventually she found what she was looking for.

"There it is." The small thorn came out easily in her fingers.

"Golly, you didn't have to do surgery or nothin?" Jason, at seven the oldest of the three, sounded disappointed.

"Is there any blood?" Clay asked eagerly.

"Blood?" Rachel cried. "You want Scooter to bleed?"

Clay hung his head. "Gee, not if it'd hurt him."

Rachel took pity and ruffled Clay's hair. "I know. You just like blood, you little vampire."

"He can't be a vampire," Jason said. "He already tried. But vampires have to stay up all night, and Mom and Dad won't let him."

"Ah." Rachel nodded soberly. "I see. Well, I guess he'll just have to be a boy."

Clay held out his hands and shrugged. "That's me. Just a boy."

Three-year-old Grant imitated Clay's pose and mimicked, "Just a boy."

Rachel tweaked Grant's nose. "If you don't start speaking for yourself instead of repeating everything everyone else says, we're going to start calling you Polly." She reached out and tickled his ribs, and the free-for-all was on.

Rachel and her three nephews rolled and shrieked and giggled across the side yard, while Scooter romped and barked and threw himself joyfully into the pile.

Rachel was the first to cry uncle. Weak with laughter, she crawled on her hands and knees away from the melee.

"Good grief, what's all the ruckus?" Trey called

as he rounded the corner of the house. "It sounds like a massacre is going on."

"It is," Rachel said breathlessly to the youngest of her three brothers. "I lost."

By the time she caught her breath, Ace was calling everyone to eat. The first round of burgers was ready and waiting. Whooping and hollering, the boys untangled themselves and raced to get a spot at the picnic tables placed end to end to allow room for everyone.

Rachel followed much more slowly, with Trey laughing at her, when Belinda called out to the boys, "Wash first!"

Figuring she needed it as much as the boys, Rachel followed them into the kitchen and took her turn at the sink.

Back outside a few minutes later, she joined her family—Donna, Stoney, and Frank were family, too—for a boisterous, fun-filled meal.

"Boy, I sure wish Cody coulda come today," Clay said.

A quick glance around the table told Rachel that the sudden silence from the adults was not her imagination. To a person, they all looked at her, then down at their food.

Rachel gave a mental shrug. There weren't all that many little boys in Wyatt County. With few job opportunities, young people moved to the city—any city—to earn an income that would support their family. Few stayed and raised children here anymore. It seemed inevitable to her that a friendship would develop between the Wilder boys and Cody Lewis.

"He had to go back to California with his dad," Clay offered.

"Is that so?" Ace asked slowly, his gaze centered on Rachel.

Ace, indeed all her brothers, had been her bulwark when Grady had run off. They'd been a solid rock of support when she'd needed it the most.

"Yeah," Jason added. "They're gonna pack up all their stuff and move back here and live at Standing Elk. That'll be cool. I like him. Even if he is just a five-year-old," he added from his lofty two-year advantage.

Jack's eyes narrowed. "They're moving back here?"

"Yes," Rachel confirmed. "I thought surely you'd all heard by now."

Trey cocked his head and eyed her sharply. "You all right with that?"

Rachel shrugged. "It's no big deal." She would make sure of it.

After Sunday with her family, Rachel came in Monday morning refreshed and ready to start a new week. She'd made it all the way through Sunday without any emergency calls. For Monday Louise had set up a string of office appointments that kept them both busy all day. Late in the morning on Tuesday she had to drive out to the Kettering place twenty miles east of town to worm their prize bull. Just after she started back to the clinic her cell phone rang. It was Louise.

"Are you on your way back?" Louise wanted to know.

"Yes. I'm about ten minutes east of town. I'll be there in fifteen or twenty minutes. What's up?"

"Colicky horse, here at the ranch."

"I'm on my way."

As Rachel hit town and drove the four miles north to the ranch, she went over the information Louise had given her over the phone. Elevated temperature, pulse and respiration. Sweating. Obviously in pain. No fresh droppings in the past few hours. No gut sounds. The only good sign was that the capillary refill of the mucous membranes was still okay. When Joe had pressed his thumb to the stallion's gum, the resultant white spot had turned pink again within three to four seconds. Not bad. Rachel would have been happier, though, with two to three seconds.

She had seen colicky horses before, both at home when she was growing up, and later at veterinary school, as well as here in the county since she'd joined the Standing Elk Clinic. She knew pretty much what to expect.

But she was not expecting the sight that greeted her when she turned off onto the ranch road and pulled up a moment later at the barn.

Grady was back. She should have known. Somehow she should have been able to prepare herself for seeing him again.

She had told herself a hundred times in the last week that seeing him would be no big deal, that she had her reactions under control.

She'd been wrong. Her racing pulse was telling her that the sight of him, knowing she was going to have to talk with him, work with him to save the horse, was a *very* big deal.

She should have known it was his horse that was in trouble. Standing Elk didn't have a stallion. Or hadn't, until now. The ranch's new owner had trailered his in from California.

He must have just arrived. His pickup was parked near the barn, with boxes and gear in the bed that reminded her yet again that he would be living in Wyatt County now. She would likely see him every day.

She could handle it. She *would* handle it.

His horse trailer was still hooked up to the bumper of his pickup. A pretty little steel-gray mare with black points stood inside the nearest corral. While Joe groomed the mare, the animal watched as Grady walked the black stallion with a white blaze along the drive between the barn and the house.

And in the front yard of the house, Cody sat wide-eyed on the grass with a small duffel bag at his side. When he spotted her, he jumped up and waved. Rachel waved back, but then centered her attention on her patient.

The stallion was one of the most beautiful she had ever seen. Or would have been, she corrected, if he wasn't in pain. He didn't want to walk with Grady, that much was obvious. He wanted to look back toward his flank and the pain in his gut. And Rachel knew that what he wanted most was to throw himself down and roll in an attempt to rid himself of the pain. Roll, and let his intestines twist up, which he didn't understand would kill him.

"Not while I'm around," Rachel muttered.

And not, she could tell, while a grim-faced Grady had a good hold on the lead line.

"Miss Rachel," Cody cried. "Sugarfoot's sick. He's got the colic. That means he can't poop."

"So I heard." She grabbed her bag and climbed out of the truck. "That's why I'm here."

"You're a vet? You gonna make him all better?"

"Yes, I am a vet, and I'm going to do my best."

"Dad says I have to stay away from him and stay in the yard 'cause Sugarfoot might accidentally hurt me while he doesn't feel good."

"Your dad's a smart man," Rachel told him. She'd wager a year's earnings that Grady didn't let Cody near the stallion without strict supervision, no matter how good the horse felt. Stallions weren't docile creatures by nature.

Rachel approached the horse, and Grady drew the animal to a halt. He gave her a nod. "Thanks for coming so quick."

"You're welcome." As she began her examination, she asked, "Any idea when this started? How's his water intake?"

"He won't drink."

That was not a good sign, but it was what Rachel expected.

"He was fine this morning, but a couple of hours ago when I stopped for gas he had stopped eating and there were no fresh droppings in his side of the trailer. I gave him a tranquilizer to relax him, but when I stopped to check on him an hour later he was worse, so I shot him full of pain killer. You can see for yourself that isn't working either."

Listening to the horse's stomach and hearing no gurgling, as there should have been if his digestive tract was working, Rachel stepped back and reached into her bag. Ordinarily she wouldn't have recommended trailering an animal with signs of colic, but she knew that wherever Grady had been, if it was an hour from here, it was the middle of nowhere. He'd been right to drive on in and get to a vet.

"What do you think?" Grady asked.

"I'm going to give him a strong sedative that will put him down and out. He'll be so relaxed he wouldn't feel it if we cut off his legs. That relaxed, everything should loosen up in there."

Grady led the horse to a clean stall in the barn and Rachel administered the sedative. In moments the big stallion was on his side and out cold.

"How long?" Grady asked.

"We'll give it about an hour to work."

"Then what?"

"Then," she said, "we take the next step."

Grady's lips twitched. "Did you bring your long gloves?" he asked.

Rachel pursed her lips but did not answer. They both knew that if there was no improvement in about an hour, she would have to reach up inside the horse and pull the compacted manure out by hand.

"By the way," Grady said. "I meant to congratulate you last week."

"For what?"

"You did it. All your life you wanted to be a vet, and now you are one. I'm glad for you."

Rachel's smile was bittersweet. "Thank you," she told him. "You wanted the same thing for yourself. I'm sorry it didn't work out."

Grady shook his head. "That was a dream. I've long since given up on dreams."

He said it so matter-of-factly that Rachel felt a little tear in her heart. She turned away and spotted Cody peeking around the edge of the barn door.

"Is he gonna be all right?" Cody asked.

Grady came to the stall door. "I hope so, pard. Aren't you supposed to be in the yard?"

Cody looked at his father anxiously. "Yes, sir."

Grady sighed. "You can come on in now. He's asleep."

Rachel watched as Cody stepped tentatively up to Grady's side at the open door of the stall.

"Can I pet him?"

"Yeah," Grady said quietly. "For a minute. Then you need to start getting your things into the house."

Cody approached the stallion's head with caution and slowly knelt. After petting the horse's sweaty neck for a minute, he got up and looked at his dad. "He's gonna be okay, Dad. Miss Rachel will make him well. Won't you?" he added, looking up at Rachel.

The faith in the boy's eyes, the sheer certainty that she could make the stallion well again, humbled her. She'd heard her fair share of wisecracks from a few of the area ranchers about a woman animal doctor. The look in Cody's eyes made her feel as if she could cure any ailment in the world.

"I'm going to do my best," she said.

"See, Dad?"

"I see," Grady said, placing his hand on his son's head. "Now go get unpacked."

"Okay. That oughta earn me a couple of cookies, ya think?"

"Not until you eat the lunch Alma's fixing you."

Rachel watched Cody scamper out of the barn and off toward the house. He was so precious, it almost hurt to look at him.

"That morning I got the call about his birth," she said quietly, "I was so hurt—"

"Rachel, don't," Grady said.

"No, I'm not...I don't mean to get into any of that. I just mean that when I heard you had a son, my first thought was that *I* was supposed to be the mother of your son, and because I wasn't, he shouldn't have been born.''

Grady wanted to close his eyes against the pain her words brought, but he couldn't. He couldn't stop looking at her. Couldn't stop hurting for both of them. All of them.

''I actually thought that,'' she admitted. ''Just for a minute. Then I felt so sick for wishing an innocent little baby hadn't been born just because I wanted him to be mine that I couldn't even look at myself in the mirror. He's so beautiful, Grady. So much like you were at his age. No matter what else I thought about you or his mother, I never, after that one minute, wished anything but good for him.''

Tell her, Grady thought. Tell her the truth. There would never be a more perfect time. She had just given him the opening he needed. There was no reason to keep the secret any longer. Not from her.

Still, he hesitated, and he wasn't sure why.

No, that wasn't true. He knew exactly why. First, the truth was something he'd never told aloud to anyone. He had guarded the secret so well that he wasn't sure he had the words with which to reveal it now. In the beginning he'd kept quiet out of necessity. Later, out of habit.

But he would have told her that day before he left town, if she'd given him the chance.

That was what hurt the most. What kept him silent now. The two of them had known and loved each other for nearly their entire lives. Not once, since he realized at age fifteen how he really felt about her, had he ever even looked at another girl, another woman. Rachel had known that. She'd known how much he loved her.

Yet all it had taken had been a single phone call from a casual friend to make her think the worst of him. To make her believe he had betrayed her. She hadn't even given him the benefit of the doubt for so much as a minute.

When he'd gone to see her, to explain, she hadn't said, "Tell me it isn't true." She hadn't said, "I know it can't be true because you would never cheat on me." She hadn't even asked, "Is it true?"

Instead, she had turned him away without a word, without giving him a chance to say anything.

He would have shouted it out to her as she'd stood there on the staircase in her home, but she'd been surrounded by all three of her brothers, and they had been more interested in her wish—that Grady get out of the house and leave—than in letting him say his piece. Besides, he couldn't have spoken the truth in front of them. There had been too much at risk.

She had spent the past five years hating him, without knowing or caring that he had even more reason to resent her.

So tell her.

But she turned away from him just then and bent to see about his horse, and the moment was lost.

It was just as well, he thought as he followed her. What's done is done.

That night Rachel couldn't sleep.

She should have been able to. She'd put in a hard, satisfying day. She'd saved a prize bull from tiny parasites, a cat from cystitis, a fancy French poodle from future unwanted pregnancies, and a beautiful stallion from colic. Not bad for a little girl who only wanted someone to save her pony.

But it was the pony-saver's son, the stallion's owner, who kept her awake tonight.

Dammit, she had to get him out of her thoughts. She'd thought for years that she had, but obviously she'd been wrong, and it was past time to do something about that. She wanted him out of her mind once and for all. She wanted to let go of the past.

Yeah, well, what was it Jack always said? "Want in one hand and spit in the other, and see which hand gets filled, kid."

Throughout the night and the days that followed, it became more than apparent to Rachel just which hand was getting filled.

Chapter Five

Grady had spent the morning on horseback helping Joe move cattle to fresh grass.

Standing Elk wasn't nearly as big an operation as the Flying Ace; it wasn't even as large as some of the medium-sized ranches in the county. Ray Lewis had purposely kept the ranch on the small side, because his main business had been the clinic. Still, the four square miles within Standing Elk's boundaries—including the eighty acres that now belonged to Joe and Alma—had to be managed every bit as carefully as the larger outfits. Even more so in some aspects, such as grazing.

The Wilders' Flying Ace butted up against the mountains, making it possible for them to move their herd to leased land at cooler, higher elevations during the summer months, sparing the grass down on the home range.

Standing Elk had no such option. The mountains were too far, and there was too much private property to cross to get to them. So they had to watch their grass with as much attention as a buzzard watching the desert floor for his supper. If the cattle ate the grass too far down, an entire pasture—acres and acres of once good grass—could be ruined for years. Forever.

So year after year they moved their cattle from one pasture to another, as he and Joe had just done.

It felt good to work cattle again. In California he'd been a horse trainer. He'd come to realize during the past few years that training horses, rather than treating their diseases and injuries, was what he wanted to do.

They said something good comes out of everything that starts out bad. Well, "they" had been right in his case. He had Cody, and he had his life's work—horse training.

Still, he had missed working cattle. They'd had only a few head of cattle on the ranch where he had worked in California, only enough to use in working the cow horses and getting them ready for sale. Today was the first time Grady had herded cattle in five years. He was home. It felt just like old times. Even his bad knee had held up pretty good, with nothing more than a twinge to remind him that his rodeo days were, if not over, at least numbered.

As he pulled the saddle from his mare an SUV came down the drive.

More old times, he thought with a twisting sensation in the pit of his stomach as Rachel climbed out of the driver's seat. For all of two seconds, he forgot. He grinned and took a step toward her. How many times in years past had she come barreling down that drive to see him?

Then he remembered. She wasn't his anymore. Hadn't been for years. If she hadn't already been within earshot he would have cussed a blue streak at his own stupidity. And at her, for showing up here instead of pulling up at the clinic. In disgust, he turned back and continued brushing Gray Ghost.

Behind him he heard Rachel walk up to the corral fence. Heard her footsteps stop.

He kept working.

Finally she spoke. "Good afternoon."

He didn't want to be rude. He'd been taught better. But dammit, why did she have to come over here? He'd been purposely staying away from the clinic. It seemed to him she could return the favor and stay away from him.

Apparently she thought differently.

He paused with the brush on Gray Ghost's back and looked over his shoulder. "What are you doing over here?"

Rachel felt the sting of a blush climb up her cheeks. This wasn't exactly the greeting she'd expected. But then, she didn't know what she'd been expecting. She didn't know what the devil she was doing here. For some reason, it had seemed like a good idea when she'd bypassed the clinic and driven toward the house and barns.

She shook her hair back from her face. Nothing to do now but brazen it out. "I was just coming back from the Johnsons' and thought I'd drop over and check on my patient."

"Is that so?"

He might as well have said, "That's weak, Rachel. Real weak." Because it was.

Brazen it out, she reminded herself. "Where is Sugarfoot?"

Grady nodded toward the small five-acre pasture south of the corrals.

Rachel followed his gaze and spotted the big black stallion beneath the trees near the back fence line.

Grady let out a shrill whistle. The stallion's head jerked up.

Rachel couldn't see from this distance, but she knew those sharp ears had swiveled toward Grady.

Grady let out two whistles this time, and the horse turned and raced across the grass, mane and tail flying out behind him like black flags.

"God, he's beautiful," she murmured.

"He is that," Grady agreed. "I'll ask again, Rachel. What are you doing here?"

"You sound as if you'd rather I'd fall off the face of the earth," she said, miffed at his tone.

"I wouldn't go that far. I just don't see the point of this little social call."

Rachel ground her teeth. "Little social call? Is that what you think this is?"

"You tell me."

"For your information, I came over here to—" To what? she asked herself.

"To what?" Grady demanded, finally coming to stand before her.

The corral fence stood between them. For all Rachel could tell, it might as well have been the Great Wall of China.

"To play games with my head?" Grady demanded. "You don't want anything to do with me

and we both know it. You made that more than clear
five years ago. Believe me, I got the message.''

"How dare you take that attitude with me, Grady
Lewis. After what you did to me, not to mention
what you did to LaVerne—the poor girl died having
your son—you've got no right to get on your high
horse with me now.''

"Et tu, Rachel?''

If a person could freeze from a blast of ice in a
man's eyes, Rachel would have been dead on the
spot. ''Me too, what?''

"Do you think like everybody else around here,
that I'm the one who beat up LaVerne that night?
That I'm the one who gave her those internal injuries
that killed her?''

"Don't be ridiculous,'' she spat. ''I know you better than that. You wouldn't hit a girl—much less a
girl about to have your baby.''

"Well, thanks for that, at least.'' His tone was
anything but thankful. ''Someday when you decide
you want the rest of the truth, you let me know.''

"The rest of the truth? I don't have to ask, thank
you very much. I know the truth. It's a little hard to
miss with a miniature version of you running around,
don't you think?''

Grady let out a snort of disgust.

His attitude was really starting to burn her.
''There's nothing you can say that can change what
you did. It was a long time ago. I came over here
today to see if we could put it behind us and maybe
be, if not friends, at least civil acquaintances. Busi-
nesslike business partners.''

Her words caught Grady off guard. He didn't
know what he'd expected her to say, but this wasn't

it, last week he'd been thinking about her share of the blame for what had happened. Last week, last year—hell, he'd been angrily laying blame at her feet thirty seconds ago.

He didn't see how the two of them could ever get beyond their past if he didn't tell her what had really happened. She might think she knew, but she had no idea of the truth. Last week he hadn't been ready to tell her. Now, maybe it was time.

"Rachel…there's something you need to know about—"

"No." She held out her hand to stop him. "There's nothing about what happened five years ago that I need to know."

"You're wrong."

She shook her head hard. "Maybe I should have said there's nothing about it that I want to hear."

"Even if—"

"I mean it, Grady, don't. We're going to have to deal with each other now and then. I don't see any way around that. Can't we just work on that, instead of a past that can't be changed?"

Grady might have pushed it, might have told her the truth whether she felt like hearing it or not, but it was obvious that she wanted as little to do with him as possible. If her mind was closed, she wouldn't believe him no matter what he said.

The honking of a horn drew their attention to the rig that was backing a horse trailer up to the stables behind the clinic.

"Looks like you've got some work to do," Grady observed.

"The Satterlys," Rachel said. "They're new to the area since you've been gone. They bought the Donnely place north of here. They have to go back East to their son's wedding in Mobile, and they're afraid their mare will foal while they're gone."

"Will she?"

"According to your father's records and theirs, she could foal a day or two before they get home. They've got somebody staying at their place to take care of the livestock while they're gone, but they haven't had much luck with foaling in the past."

"And they're nervous."

"Yeah."

"Wouldn't the mare be better off at home on familiar ground this close to foaling?"

"Normally, yes. But they lost this one's dam during foaling. Aside from being understandably gun-shy, they bottle-fed this filly. She's definitely a people horse, and she's not particular. She loves everybody, and she's not happy being left alone. I better get up there. I'll...see you."

"Yeah." Grady stood at the corral fence and watched her drive up the gravel road to the clinic.

Another chance denied. Another opportunity lost.

He turned back to his mare. "Gray Ghost, I give up. The lady wants nothing to do with me. Her mind's been made up about me for years. No sense bothering her with anything so trivial as the truth, huh, girl?"

Gray Ghost nickered softly and shook her head.

"Yeah," Grady told her, taking a stroke down her back with the brush. "That's what I thought."

After leaving Grady, Rachel spent the next forty-five minutes assuring the Satterlys that Maggie M'Darling was in good hands, that Rachel would care for her as if she were her own prized mare. And she would.

But as she'd told Grady, Dr. Ray's records indicated that the mare wasn't due to foal for at least several days, if not a good couple of weeks. Not that the foal could read those records. It might decide to come at any time, so Rachel would keep an eye on the mare. But for now there was no need to keep a twenty-four hour watch. The mare was exhibiting none of the usual signs that foaling was imminent.

That decided, Rachel and Louise locked up the clinic at six o'clock that evening and headed back to town.

Knowing there was nothing in her cupboards that she wanted to eat, Rachel stopped at Biddle's Grocery on Main to find something to fix for supper. As she perused the meat counter, her mind was split between Maggie M'Darling and her visit to Grady. The visit she shouldn't have made.

She should have stayed away from him, and she would in the future. As she repeated that vow to herself she grabbed a package of pork chops and turned to go.

She hadn't realized anyone was behind her until she ran smack into Sheriff Martin's broad barrel of a chest.

"Oh," she cried in surprise as she stepped back and regained her balance. "I'm sorry. I didn't know you were there."

"That's quite all right, Rachel. You looked like you had a lot on your mind."

She wagged her package of pork chops. "Important stuff, all right. Supper."

The sheriff eyed her critically. "You're sure that's all? Is everything all right out there at the clinic?"

"Of course it is." Rachel's back stiffened. She didn't know what was coming, but she had the feeling she wasn't going to like it.

"That Lewis boy isn't causing you any trouble, is he?"

Rachel blinked. "Lewis boy?"

"You know who I mean, Rachel. Grady."

"What about him?"

"Come on now, Rachel. I meant what I said the other day after the funeral. Now that he's back, any girl in this county who's not careful could end up dead like my LaVerne."

Rachel blinked again, slower this time, and very deliberately. "Sheriff Martin, I don't believe you said that."

He ignored her comment. "Everybody around here knows how sweet you used to be on him. That makes you more vulnerable to him than anyone. You be careful around him, Rachel."

"Sheriff Martin, I—"

"I'm not telling you anything your own brothers wouldn't if they were me, or that your own daddy wouldn't if he was still alive."

Rachel felt her fingernails pierce the thin plastic wrapping and gouge into the raw meat beneath. It was all she could do to keep from whacking the man in the head with her supper. "Sheriff Martin, I have the utmost respect for the title of County Sheriff, and I'm sorrier than I can say about what happened to LaVerne."

"I appreciate that."

"But you are not my brother, nor my father, and

whatever I decide to do or not do with Grady Lewis or anyone else is none of your business. Good day, Sheriff.''

As she marched away from a flushed and fuming Gene Martin, standing in the meat aisle, Rachel was scarcely aware of the three witnesses to their little scene. She was so mad she wanted to spit. No, she wasn't mad, she was *furious*. How *dare* that man talk about Grady that way?

At the checkout stand she slammed her pork chops down on the conveyor belt and reached into her purse for her wallet.

The checker, one of the Haskin girls, frowned at the package. ''This package is torn. Let me have someone bring up another one for you.''

''No,'' Rachel said, trying to rein in her anger. This poor girl didn't deserve it. ''No, thanks. I tore it myself, by accident. It's fine. Really.''

Where did the man get the gall, Rachel wondered as she paid for her purchase and stomped out of the store. If he'd say something like that to her, who else was he saying it to? What nerve! What…what… ooooh!

Late that night Grady found himself too restless to sleep. He wandered the house in the dark, checked on Cody a dozen times until he feared he would wake the boy if he looked in on him again. Finally, in desperation, he let himself out the patio door and strolled into the backyard.

The night air was cool, with the sweet smell of freshly cut grass covered in dew. The sky was a mass of tiny diamonds on black velvet.

I know the truth. It's a little hard to miss with a

*miniature version of you running around, don't you
think?*

Oh, Rachel, he thought. You don't know. You just
don't know.

How could he still care so much what she thought?
How could he still feel that old yearning deep down
inside every time he saw her?

He wouldn't try again to tell her the truth. The
only person who would benefit now from the truth
would be him. It would get him off the hook with
Rachel. Maybe. If she didn't outright murder him for
not finding a way to tell her five years ago.

He bent his head back and faced the night sky and
listened to the shrill sound of crickets in the grass.
He should have found a way to tell her back then.
He could have called her. He could have gotten to
her somehow when her brothers weren't around. So
maybe he had no real right to the resentment he'd
been tasting lately.

And maybe coming back here to live hadn't been
such a bright idea. But he'd done it, and by God, he
was staying.

He strolled around the side of the house and saw
the clinic squatting beneath the security light up the
road. Before he realized his intent, he was walking
toward it and around the side to the corrals.

Rachel had left the stall door open so the Satterlys'
mare had access to the corral at will. For now the
animal must have preferred the outdoors. She nickered softly and stretched her neck over the top rail
to be petted.

Grady was glad to oblige. "You're a sweetheart,
aren't you, girl?"

Her responding nicker sounded to him as though she said, "Of course I am."

Grady laughed. Slowly, so as not to startle her, he climbed the fence. She stood patiently and let him run his hands down her side. "That foal of yours isn't going to surprise us tonight, is it?"

This time she shook her head. "No."

"Atta girl." He gave her a final pat on the shoulder, then went back over the fence and walked slowly home in the starlight.

At about 1:00 a.m. he took a final look out his bedroom window before going to bed. His room faced north, toward the drive and the clinic. He was just releasing the edge of the curtain and turning away when a long shaft of light stabbed through the darkness.

A car had turned off the highway and into the drive.

Grady waited and watched. It wasn't unheard of for someone to decide they were headed the wrong way on the highway and use the Standing Elk drive as a turnaround. But they wouldn't keep driving toward the clinic, as this car did.

He could tell now that it was a car, a small red one. It pulled up at the clinic, and the headlights winked out. Grady was turning away again, ready to race back up the drive to see what the hell was going on—nobody had any business messing around the clinic this late at night—when the interior light of the car flashed on and the driver opened the door and climbed out.

Black hair drank in the glow from the utility light and reflected it back.

It was a woman. On the small side, slender. And familiar.

"Hello, Rachel," he whispered.

"Hello, Maggie M'Darling." Rachel stroked the soft muzzle and smiled. "I know you didn't need me to come check on you tonight, but I was restless. I thought maybe you wouldn't mind a friendly visit."

In truth, it was Rachel who needed the friendly visit. She had fled from the tangled covers on her bed, or more accurately, the thoughts of a certain man who haunted her mind.

Yet even here she felt him. It was an odd sensation. During the years of his absence, she had managed to disassociate him from the clinic. Yet now she felt as if she'd walked into a room he had just left. Something in the air, a scent perhaps that was too subtle for her conscious mind to register, but picked up by her senses nonetheless. She fancied she could smell his aftershave.

Ridiculous. He probably didn't even still use that brand, after all this time. That scent that had always made her close her eyes and inhale, made her want to nuzzle his neck, nibble his jaw. Eat him alive. She remembered that smell now as if he were here next to her. Sharp and tangy, yet sweet and subtle.

She knew other men who used that same fragrance—her brother Trey, for one—but it never smelled quite the same on another man as it did on Grady.

"Oh, Maggie." She rested her head on the mare's warm neck. The haunting fragrance seemed stronger. "What am I going to do? I can't seem to get him out of my mind. I thought I was free of him, until he came back.''

The mare bobbed her head, in effect stroking the side of Rachel's face.

"Yeah, I know," Rachel answered. "He is kinda unforgettable, isn't he? But how can I still have such...warm...is that the word? Warm thoughts? About a man who hurt me so badly?''

As she feared, the mare had no answer.

A heavy sigh eased from between Rachel's lips. "Well, thanks for listening, anyway.''

Rachel went home then, but the next night, she came back. And the night after that.

Grady didn't go back the following nights to check on the mare, but he stood at his window and waited to see Rachel. She came every night, between midnight and one. She never stayed long, never even turned on the lights, but she came.

She was going to wear herself out, he thought. She showed up every morning at eight or earlier. She worked hard all day, and as far as he was concerned, she wasn't getting enough sleep.

And you are, pal?

Yeah, well...

Rachel's jaw nearly cracked on a yawn. She hoped Louise hadn't seen her or there would be a lecture, for sure. It was just four o'clock in the afternoon. A little early to start yawning.

Rachel didn't need a lecture. She knew she wasn't getting enough sleep, but that unconscious state eluded her each night until she felt compelled to get up, get out, move. Do something. So she drove out to the clinic to visit the mare. By all indications, tonight would be the last time she would have even the lame excuse she had planned if anyone asked—that she was checking on the mare.

"Pathetic," she muttered to herself.

"Did you say something?" Louise asked from the doorway.

"Just talking to myself."

"How's our mare doing? Is she ready to foal yet?"

Rachel looked over at Louise and smiled. "She's waxing, and her calcium and magnesium took a big jump today over yesterday."

"Tonight, then?"

"I'd say so."

"If you're going to stay with her, why don't you run on home and get a nap and something to eat now, then? We don't have any more appointments this afternoon."

Rachel blinked. "How did that happen?"

Louise rolled her eyes. "It happened because we had this afternoon booked to spay both of the Hensleys' rottweilers, but they got cold feet and canceled."

"The rottweilers?"

"The Hensleys, smarty. They said they wanted to think about it some more. They might want to let each of them have a litter before having them spayed."

"Just what we need in this county. Two more litters of puppies."

"No kidding. So, the rest of the afternoon is free. Get out of here for a while, why don't you."

Rachel nodded. "I think I will. Thanks. Don't wait

on me. I won't be back until around dark. I doubt Maggie will get serious about foaling until after that.''

Louise murmured in agreement and followed Rachel out of the small exam room. "Have you seen Grady lately?" the woman asked.

Just the sound of his name set butterflies dancing in Rachel's stomach. Or maybe it was frogs jumping. "No," was all she said. "I'll see you tomorrow."

Grady realized that this was the night. First, because Rachel was so early—it was just after dark—and second, she had turned the lights on in the small stable behind the clinic. Maggie M'Darling would foal tonight.

He held out until midnight, then he couldn't stand it any longer. He brewed a pot of coffee and filled the thermos. Then he went to the magnet board and moved his marker to the clinic.

It was a system he and Cody had designed last year. Sometimes Grady had been needed in the middle of the night if there was an emergency with one of the horses in his care. He didn't want to wake Cody and drag him along to the barn in the middle of the night, and there was usually no one handy to come watch the boy.

Grady never went out of sight of the house while Cody was there alone, no matter what the emergency was. The magnet board contained a rough drawing of the ranch. The round red magnet represented Grady. He put the magnet over whichever area of the ranch he'd been called to—the barn, the pasture, the corral.

They had rules. If Grady had to go outside after

Cody was asleep, Grady's rule was to leave enough lights on so Cody could see his way to the kitchen, and he was to place the magnet so Cody would know where he was.

Cody's rules were that if he woke in the middle of the night and couldn't find his dad, he was to turn on his bedroom and the front porch lights so Grady would know he was up, and he was to check the magnet board. He was not to go outside, nor was he to open the door to anyone for any reason, not even for someone he knew—unless the house was on fire. If he got scared, or just wanted to hear Grady's voice, he knew how to speed-dial the cell phone that never left Grady's belt.

Most people would say Cody was too young for such a system, but he'd grown up on a ranch, with older kids for playmates. They'd all had their chores, and Cody was extremely responsible for one so young.

He was also a sound sleeper. Grady had used the board half a dozen times in the past year, but so far Cody had yet to wake in the night and find him gone.

They'd had to draw a new map, of course, when they'd moved here. Cody had helped him, so the boy knew what everything was on the board.

Confident that Cody would be fine, and that he himself would be able to keep the house in sight, Grady picked up the thermos and let himself out the back door.

Rachel finished wrapping the mare's tail in a two-inch wide strip of clean flannel to keep it out of the way.

"There you go, girl." She stroked Maggie's side

and felt the tenseness of the muscles there. "All washed and wrapped and ready to foal. Now, all we need is the foal, huh?"

She heard approaching footsteps. Without looking, she knew who it was.

"It's all right, girl," she murmured to the mare. "It's just Grady. He likes horses. Knows all about them. I bet he'll like you." Then she raised her voice to a normal tone. "It's okay, Grady. You won't upset her."

Grady stopped outside the large foaling stall and looked in. "I saw the light. How's she doing?"

"She's doing fine." Rachel was amazed and pleased to realize that her nerves weren't dancing just because Grady was near, as they had in the past. "Classical stage one restlessness, lying down and getting up, pawing at the bedding. She's just now starting to sweat, aren't you, girl?"

"I brought coffee," Grady offered.

Rachel faced him with a deadpan expression. "She's not allowed to have caffeine."

Grady shrugged. "It's just as well. I wasn't going to let her drink out of my cup anyway. If you want to share yours with her..."

Rachel smiled. It felt good to smile at him. "No, thanks. She likes sugar in hers. I take mine black."

Grady unscrewed the cap and poured her a cup.

As he handed it to her, Rachel closed her eyes and sniffed the steam. "Wonderful. Thank you."

"You're welcome."

Rachel blew on her coffee, then took a sip, searching her mind for something safe they could talk about.

Grady beat her to it when he spoke. "Fourth of

July's coming up. Does Hope Springs still have a parade?''

Thank you, Grady.

"Parade, rodeo, barbecue, dance, games, craft booths, you name it, we still do it. You're going, aren't you?''

"Thought I would. Cody will get a kick out of it. Is the clinic going to have an entry in the parade the way it used to?''

Rachel blew a puff of air that made her bangs flutter. "I hadn't thought of that. I've missed the last few Independence Days.''

"That happens when you cram eight years of school into seven.''

Surprised, Rachel looked at him. "How did you know about that?''

"I can count. Besides, Dad told me what you were doing.''

She made a humming noise low in her throat. They were about to tread on dangerous ground, and she didn't want that. "Well, you're the majority partner around here. What do you suggest we do about the parade?''

Grady shrugged, took a sip. "I hadn't thought about it. I just wondered. Dad usually just drove the clinic rig with a few streamers tied on the back bumper.''

"With David, and you before you left, riding on a trailer, throwing candy to the kids. David always had a dog with him, too.''

Grady chuckled. "With those stupid elk antlers tied on the poor dog's head. Wonder what ever happened to those antlers.''

"Gee.'' She grinned. "I wonder.''

"What?" he asked, cocking his head.

Rachel laughed. "You just walked right beneath them."

Grady turned and looked. There, over the doorway to the stables, hung the papier-mâché antlers David had made one year in school. "I'll be damned."

"We could do something similar," Rachel said. "Maybe use the antlers somehow, or think of something new. But it'll probably be up to you and Louise to drive, because I promised months ago that I'd ride with the family and will have to race back to the end of the line if I'm going to ride in the clinic's entry."

"Oh, yeah." A slight smile curved his lips. "The famous Flying Ace riders. Do the kids ride, too?"

"Try and keep them out," she answered with a laugh. "I heard talk last Sunday of the three of them entering the stick-horse races at the arena just before the rodeo. That is, if Jason and Clay don't decide they're too old. Will you and Joe enter the team roping, the way you used to do?"

Grady shrugged. "Hadn't thought about it."

"He'd love it if you did. He's missed it. Swears he won't ride with anyone but you."

"Yeah?"

"Yeah."

He nodded. "I didn't know. Thanks for telling me."

"You're welcome." Rachel started to speak—there was a question nagging at her, no, more than one.

"What?"

She glanced at him, then shook her head.

"Come on," he coaxed quietly. "You've obviously got something on your mind."

She shrugged. "Just something I'm curious about, that's all. You can tell me it's none of my business."

"And I might."

That was encouraging. She shouldn't have said anything.

"What is it?" he asked.

He seemed so open and accessible just now. And she felt so calm. She felt none of the tension or anxiety she usually felt around him. Did that mean she was truly, finally, putting the past behind her?

"I don't want to rake up the past," she told him.

"That's what you're curious about? The past?"

"Not *that* past," she said in a rush. "I don't see any point in dredging all that up. What I'm curious about is…"

"Come on, Rachel, spill it."

She looked at him for a long moment, then smiled. "I just can't imagine how you managed a newborn baby."

His single, short laugh was traced with irony. "Who says I did?"

"No, I mean it. You'd never even been around babies, and all of a sudden, there you were."

"Yeah, there I was, scared as hell that I'd do something wrong, hold him wrong, feed him wrong. A nurse at the hospital gave me a crash course in diaper-changing and bottle-feeding, and the rest was learn-as-you-go."

"Well, you must have learned. You both survived."

"Barely," he said with a small smile. "I figured he'd survive, but I wasn't so sure about me."

Rachel laughed. "Big, bad Grady Lewis, changing

diapers, walking a crying baby in the middle of the night.''

''That was me.''

Rachel's smile faded. Sadness slowly seeped through her bones. She envied him the experience. She couldn't say it aloud, but she envied him. The baby should have been hers. They should have experienced all those things together. The diaper changing, the feeding, the teething, the first steps.

Oh, God, she was going to start crying.

She was saved from disgracing herself when Maggie M'Darling chose that moment to lower herself onto the thick straw bedding and lie flat on her side.

''Here we go.'' Shaking off the sadness, Rachel handed her cup back to Grady and let excitement fill her. ''Stage two parturition.'' A moment later the mare's water broke. ''Atta girl, Maggie, you're doing great, girl.''

The mare whinnied on a hard contraction and looked at Rachel with liquid, pain-filled eyes.

''I know, girl, but it won't be long now and you'll have a beautiful baby.'' Slowly, so as not to worry or startle, Rachel moved close and knelt in the fluid-soaked straw.

The mare strained on another hard contraction.

Rachel strained with her.

Then, ''There. I see a hoof. Good girl, Maggie, it's coming, girl.''

And then, in a rush, it was there. Or, half of it, at least. With the head, neck, shoulders and both front legs of the foal out, but the hind legs still in the birth canal, the contraction eased and the mare paused to get her breath.

''That's it, Maggie M'Darling. Oh, aren't you

clever! Just one more push now, and we'll know if you've got a colt or a filly.''

In less than a moment, the push came, one final, hard effort from the mare, and the foal's hindquarters slid free.

"There you go. No hiplock for you, eh, Maggie? Oh, and isn't he beautiful.''

"A colt?'' Grady asked. From where he stood outside the stall, with the lighting she'd purposely kept dim, and with Rachel in his way, he couldn't see.

"That's right. A little-boy horse.''

"Is that what they call them in veterinary school?''

She heard the laughter in his voice. "Actually, one professor called them horse puppies.''

"Hmm. Cost you a lot, that kind of education?''

"You're just jealous.'' She could have bitten off her own tongue the second the words were out. He, too, had wanted to become a vet, but because of— well, he hadn't been able to finish his education. She'd just rubbed salt into his wound. A self-inflicted wound, to be sure, she reminded herself. But her comment had to have hurt.

"No, actually I'm not,'' he said easily. "I think I'm happier training horses than I would be doctoring them.''

Rachel used a clean, soft rag to wipe the foal's nose. "Really?''

"Really.''

She sat back on her heels with outward patience to wait for the mare to rest a minute, then rise, or for the foal to struggle, either of which would break the umbilicus. After that the mare would clean the foal, and the foal would take a few spills climbing up onto those impossibly spindly legs on its way to nurse. Then, sometime after that, the placenta would come.

From the corner of her eye she saw Grady reach for the clipboard she'd hung on a nail on the outside of the stall. He checked his watch, then started making notes.

She would go over them and add her own notes, but seeing that he'd been raised by her mentor, had in fact grown up at this clinic, she felt confident that his notes would prove accurate and complete.

He stayed with her through those magical moments when the mare stood and started cleaning the foal, when the newborn colt struggled comically onto wobbly legs, only to tumble to the straw, then start over until finally he gained a tentative balance. Stayed through those first insecure steps, the first nuzzling for milk. Stayed until nearly an hour later when the mare delivered the placenta and Rachel examined it to make sure it was intact, that no portions had been detached to cause endometritis or laminitis.

He kept her fueled with coffee and small talk, and she was glad he was there.

And Grady was glad to be there. He was glad for the opportunity to see her in action, so to speak, without the distracting stress of it being his own animal she was working on. She was calm, confident, and from the little he'd seen so far, competent. He'd bet his lucky horseshoe that his dad had been busting with pride the day she came to work for him as a doctor of veterinary medicine.

But Grady had meant what he'd told her earlier. He wasn't sorry that he'd dropped out of college. He'd found his life's work, and that was training horses. The things he'd learned in California had helped him build a good reputation in the training business. He intended to build on it now that he was his own boss and could do things his own way.

Chapter Six

The next day after work Rachel was restless. She was tired and she had an early call to make tomorrow morning. She should spend the evening with her feet up and her mind lost in a novel. Instead, she found herself on the highway headed south out of town toward the Flying Ace.

She had the windows down; the wind whipped her hair around, but she didn't care. She wanted the wind. She wanted speed. The little sports car was loaded with power, and she wanted to let it loose.

But she didn't relish getting stopped for speeding, especially if Sheriff Martin was patrolling tonight.

With a sigh, she kept to the speed limit. Still, it was all right. The sun was behind the mountains and twilight settled gently over the rangeland. To Rachel, this underpopulated corner of the world was the most beautiful place she'd ever seen. It was, quite simply, home. That, to her, said it all.

When she arrived at the ranch she found Belinda and the kids alone at the house. She spent a few minutes in the living room with the kids, then joined Belinda in the kitchen. The kitchen table was the family's main gathering area.

"Where's Ace?" Rachel asked.

Belinda rolled her eyes. "It's poker night. They're all gathered around Jack's kitchen table pretending to be he-men."

Rachel grinned. "What's the matter? Wouldn't they let you play?"

Belinda snorted. "Not since I won Ace's favorite Winchester from him last winter. He's never forgiven me. Neither has Trey, for that matter. Number Three wanted it for himself."

"Don't mind Trey. He's always wanted that rifle, but all he wants to do is hang it on his wall and tell everybody he won it off Ace."

"Yeah, unlike me, huh?" Belinda laughed. "Frank was worried that I wanted to outline my name in bullet holes across the side of the barn, until Ace reminded him I couldn't hit the side of the barn."

Both women laughed.

"And Donna?" Rachel asked, noting that the housekeeper wasn't around.

"She drove into town for the evening. I don't expect her back for a couple of hours. Why don't I put on some coffee?" Belinda offered. "You don't usually drive all the way out here after work in the middle of the week. You look like a woman with something on her mind."

Not admitting anything, Rachel pulled out a chair at the table and sat down. "Thanks. Coffee sounds good."

Belinda started a fresh pot brewing, then leaned against the counter to wait on it. "It wouldn't have anything to do with a certain old flame who's moved back to town, would it?"

Rachel sighed. She could dodge Belinda for a few more minutes, but to what good? Belinda had a mind like a steel trap, sharp and lethal, and once it got hold of something, it wouldn't let go. And why should she dodge? Hadn't she come out here to talk to someone? She might not have admitted it to herself, but that was the truth. And she would certainly rather talk to Belinda, who had only recently met Grady, than to one of her brothers, who'd been present that day they'd learned of his involvement with LaVerne.

"A certain old flame," she said with disgust. "Try *the* old flame. The only flame, old or otherwise, I've ever had."

"And now he's back in town."

"Yes."

"And you still have feelings for him?"

Rachel studied the tabletop with an intensity bordering on obsession. "I have no business feeling *anything* for him after the way he did me."

"That wasn't what I asked," Belinda said with a soft smile. "But I guess you answered me anyway, didn't you? Those old embers are still there, huh?"

"Mom?" Clay said from the doorway to the hall. "Our mouths are bored. Can we have some ice cream?"

Belinda glanced at the clock on the wall. "I guess that could be arranged."

Rachel helped her dish up chocolate ice cream for three little boys. And two women. They made the boys come to the table for theirs. Belinda and Rachel were just sitting down to join them when the back door banged open and all three of Rachel's brothers clomped into the kitchen.

"Ah ha!" Ace cried. "See? I was right. They're eating."

Belinda rolled her eyes. "You guys can smell food a mile away."

"Where's ours?" Trey demanded.

Belinda spooned up a bite of ice cream and motioned toward the freezer. "Help yourselves."

Ace kissed the top of Belinda's head and made for the freezer. "That's what I love about married life. A woman to wait on me hand and foot."

It was hard to tell who snorted the loudest at that blatant lie.

With narrowed eyes that promised retribution, Belinda smiled around her spoonful of ice cream. "Wrong wife, Slick."

Ace grunted and started dishing up ice cream for himself. Jack and Trey were on their own.

"So what are you doing out here tonight, Little Sis?"

"Her house is on fire," Clay stated calmly.

"*What?*" all three Wilder men cried.

Rachel frowned at Clay. "My house isn't on fire, honey. Why would you think that?"

Clay shrugged and licked his spoon. "What else could it be? You was talkin' about flames and embers and all."

With all three of her brothers staring at her and waiting for an explanation, Rachel felt another set of flames, this time dancing across her cheeks. "That was, uh, just a figure of speech," she managed.

Ace's gaze sharpened. "As in *old flame,* maybe?"

Rachel took her time spooning up another bite of ice cream. "Nonsense."

Nothing more was said about flames and embers until the kids finished their ice cream and went back to the living room.

Then Ace pounced. "You're not seeing Lewis again, are you?"

"Ace," Belinda cautioned.

"You weren't here," he said, his voice hard. "You didn't see what that jerk did to her."

"No," Belinda said calmly. "I didn't. And unless Rachel wants to talk about it, it's none of our business." She eyed her husband and his brothers. "None of ours."

"The hell it isn't," Ace said. "I'll be damned if I'll stand by and watch her get involved with him again so he can—"

"Excuse me?" Rachel interjected between clenched teeth. "First of all, big brother, nobody said anything about anyone getting involved. Second, I'm a grown woman. My life is my business, and not yours."

"You're not going to start seeing Grady Lewis again." Ace made it a statement, not a question. A statement that sounded suspiciously like an order. "I don't want you anywhere around him."

"I see him every day," Rachel told him with a toss of her head. "It's kind of hard not to, since I work right there on his ranch, and we're partners in the clinic."

"You know that's not what I meant," Ace said, totally unrepentant.

Rachel sighed. "I know you love me and you don't want to see me get hurt, and I love you for that. But there's no way I can avoid being around him now and then, and I don't intend to try." She stood and grabbed her purse from the counter. "There are a lot worse men in this county I could be seeing than Grady Lewis."

"Not in my book," Ace muttered.

"You read your book," she said tightly, "and I'll read mine. Good night. Thanks for the ice cream, Belinda."

"Dammit, Rachel," Ace called as she rushed out the back door.

"Way to go, Slick," Belinda said.

Ace started to go after his sister, but his wife's words stopped him.

"Don't you dare," Belinda snapped. "What are you trying to do, drive her straight into Grady Lewis's arms?"

"Of course not," he protested.

"Then leave her alone."

"She's right, you know," Jack said easily. "Telling Rachel not to do something is the same as daring her to do it."

"Like waving a red flag in front of a bull," Trey added.

"Oh, great." Ace threw his hands up. "We're supposed to just stand back and watch her get hurt again?"

"Maybe he won't hurt her this time," Belinda offered.

All three men stared at her in shocked protest.

"He cheated on her," Trey cried.

"Got another girl pregnant while he was engaged to Rachel."

"And the way I hear it," Belinda offered, "he lost everything he ever cared about because of that one foolish act."

Trey looked thoughtful. "He lost Rachel, that's for sure, and there's no denying he was crazy about her."

"Didn't he also lose his home, his family, the veterinary degree he was after? Every friend he ever had? Don't get me wrong—I'd like to wring his neck for hurting Rachel, and I make no excuses for anyone who can't remain faithful. But it seems to me he's paid a steeper price than most for his mistake. It might just be that he's grown up some since then."

"I don't believe you," Ace said, his eyes wide. "This, from Ms. Feminist herself? He cheated on her, and you're saying we should forget it?"

"I'm saying it's up to Rachel. The rest of us should back off and let her find her own way."

"Right after I pay him a little visit," Ace muttered.

Belinda narrowed her eyes. "Over my dead body, cowboy."

Rachel couldn't believe she'd done that. Not only had she walked out on her family, she'd come perilously close—if not over the line—to defending Grady. How could she defend the man who had ripped her heart to shreds?

The question echoed over and over in her mind as she ground her teeth and raced down the gravel ranch road toward the highway. If she hadn't needed her foot on the gas pedal, she would have used it to kick herself in the rear.

Not only was she angry, she was worried.

Scared was more like it. And confused.

For a few minutes the other night during the foaling, she had been at ease around Grady. It had seemed just then that perhaps they could become friends. It did not hit her until later, as the sun was coming up and she had been climbing into bed for a nap, how much she wanted his friendship. How much she wanted more than friendship.

How could a woman be so stupid? It was like asking to pet the snake that just bit her. Hadn't he nearly destroyed her once? Even if all she wanted was friendship, a friend was someone to trust. How could she ever trust a man who had betrayed her? And why would she even want to?

But she did want to. She finally had to admit that to herself. She wanted to trust Grady. Wanted to be friends. But she knew that she couldn't be around him without wanting more. Not unless he had changed more than she'd seen. Or unless she had.

He was a good father to Cody. A wonderful father. He loved that boy something fierce. That had to say something about the man he'd become, didn't it?

And that she was even thinking this way had to say something about the deterioration of her own will and mind. There had been more than one time during the past five years when she'd sworn that if she ever got Grady Lewis in her sights again there would be hell to pay.

Now, it seemed as though she was the one paying it.

Forced to slow for the cattle guard and the turn onto the highway, Rachel also slowed her racing thoughts. As her car bumped gently over the iron poles, her mind bumped easily back to the past. To the Grady she had known before her world fell apart.

Before he tore it apart, you mean, and don't you forget it.

It was getting dark now. Her headlights stabbed a path down the blacktop. The wind rushing in through her open windows grew colder as she picked up speed.

When she thought of the Grady she used to know—the boy, the young man she had loved and who had loved her—she didn't understand how he could have changed so much. Never would she have dreamed he would betray her. He had always been so open and honest with her, all the years they'd grown up together. He *had* loved her. If there was anything she believed, it was that.

How could he have changed? He'd had such integrity. A real stand-up kind of guy who fought for what he believed in.

Yet he'd slept with LaVerne Martin, and then gone off to college with Rachel, and for the next nine months he acted as if nothing had changed, as if he still loved her with every breath he took.

For five years the questions had haunted her, the answers eluding, always out of her grasp. How *could* he?

Ask him.

She couldn't do that. She would die if she had to listen to him tell about being with LaVerne, even in the most abstract terms. She would just curl up in a little bitty ball and die.

Loose LaVerne, of all people.

"Shame on you," she muttered to herself. LaVerne had paid with her life for her indiscretion. She didn't deserve to be remembered with such a derogatory name. Rachel wouldn't pretend she had ever liked the girl, but she had no business denigrating her when she wasn't here to defend herself.

But Grady's here, and he tried to defend himself. You wouldn't listen.

Defend himself? That wasn't really what he'd said. He'd said he wanted to tell her the truth.

There was no truth he could tell her that would make any difference. The truth was, he betrayed her. He fathered a child—a beautiful little boy whom Rachel already loved—with another woman. He'd left town. He'd stayed gone for five years. He'd destroyed her life, her dreams. Her heart.

Those were the truths. If she had to listen to him tell her about being with LaVerne...no, he could keep his *truth*.

Why, then, couldn't she stop thinking about him? Why did the old pull feel stronger every time she saw him? There were times when she thought it was at least as strong if not stronger than what she'd felt as a teenager.

And there hid another truth. She'd never gotten over him. That was why she'd never been able to bring herself to get involved with another man. Why she'd used school to keep herself too busy for anything but an occasional casual date.

A flash of light drew her gaze to her rearview mirror. Some portion of her mind had been aware that a car was coming up behind her, but she hadn't paid any attention. She should have. The light she saw now was red and flashing.

"Oh, hell." The needle on her speedometer was dancing boldly on eighty. "Oh, hell."

She slowed and pulled off onto the shoulder of the road and waited.

"Late-night veterinary emergency?"

Rachel looked up into the startlingly handsome face of Undersheriff Dane Powell. She'd met Dane when she came home on spring break a couple of months ago, shortly after Sheriff Martin hired him. Sometimes she caught herself wondering why she couldn't be attracted to him. He was gorgeous in a hard-edged sort of way. With that black hair, those blue eyes, those chiseled features, you could put him in a room with her three brothers and a stranger would be hard-pressed to pick out the one who wasn't a Wilder.

He seemed honest and dependable. She'd seen him back down three angry drunks at once without breaking a sweat, so she knew he was tough.

But from the moment they met, she'd felt a sort of sisterly affection for him that surprised and confused her. And he treated her as though she were a sister. They were friends, and that's all they would ever be. And it was a crying shame.

She gave him a twisted smile. "If I said it was an emergency, I'd be lying."

He flashed his flashlight into the car. "At least you've got your seat belt on. That'll come in handy, maybe, when a deer or an elk steps out in front of you. Of course, a little tin can like this, it won't matter much. You'll all be totaled—the animal, the car, and you.''

Rachel rolled her eyes. ''And at sixty-five I'll be ever so much safer.''

Dane pursed his lips. ''At sixty-five you won't get charged with slaughtering animals out of season. It'll be a comfort to your surviving family members. You gonna slow down?''

''Yes, sir.'' She gave him a sheepish grin. ''I wasn't deliberately speeding. I just wasn't paying attention.''

He shook his head, but she saw the twinkle in his eye. ''A smart college girl like you, I thought for sure you could come up with a better excuse than that old cliché.''

''I promise to come up with something better the next time.''

''The next time, you're getting a ticket, no matter how good your excuse.''

She smiled in gratitude that he wasn't giving her a ticket this time. ''Yes, sir. And Dane, thanks.''

''Don't mention it.'' He smiled back. ''I mean, really, don't mention it. I'm *supposed* to give you a ticket this time.''

''My lips are sealed.''

''Just slow down.''

''I promise.''

What a doll, Rachel thought when she pulled back onto the highway and carefully watched her speed. Why couldn't she fall for a man like him?

The next day was Thursday, and Louise had booked a series of in-clinic small-animal appointments. Rachel saw two wormy cats and a wormy dog, had Jimmy dip two dogs to rid them of fleas, diagnosed a case of ear mites in an angry tom cat, and scratched her head over a pet gopher snake that had quit eating.

"I don't know, Bobby," she told the young owner. "I'll have to study up on this one. Have you seen him eat anything strange lately?"

"Strange?"

"Something he's not used to eating."

Bobby shrugged. "I don't guess."

Rachel let out a low hum and studied the file Louise had given her. "You're, uh, not still feeding him oatmeal, are you?"

"Ma'am?"

"Dr. Ray made a note the last time you brought Gopher in. It says you'd been feeding him oatmeal."

Bobby swallowed and blinked up at her. "It does?"

"I'll bet he told you not to do that, didn't he?"

The boy swallowed again. "Uh, maybe."

"Have you eaten any live mice lately?"

His eyes bugged out. "Yuck. Not me."

"Why not?"

"Yuck!"

"It's not exactly people food, is it?"

Bobby shook his head hard.

"Well, oatmeal is not snake food. It makes him sick." It constipated the heck out of the poor snake was what it did. But according to Dr. Ray's notes, the, uh, situation would pass on its own.

"If I promise not to feed him oatmeal again—"

"Or any other people food—"

"Can I take him home with me?"

"I think Gopher would prefer that to staying here, don't you?"

"Thanks, Dr. Wilder."

By the time Louise saw Bobby and his mother and Gopher out the door it was noon.

Louise circled the counter and stood before the front window to watch their last client of the morning leave. "No more appointments until three," she told Rachel. "How's the snake?"

"Overfed and constipated," Rachel muttered. "You could have warned me."

Louise chuckled.

Jimmy came out of the back room with his backpack slung over one shoulder. The seventeen-year-old fancied himself a writer. The backpack, Rachel knew, was crammed with spiral notebooks, yellow legal pads, pens, pencils, a battered copy of *Roget's Thesaurus,* and an even more battered copy of Strunk and White's *Elements of Style.* And, to hear his mother tell it, a change of clothes and the kitchen sink.

"I've finished mopping in the kennel," he told Rachel. "Anything else I need to do?"

"Did you clean up after the mess of flea-dipping?"

"Yep."

"I guess that's it, then. Got a hot date tonight?" At seventeen, Jimmy also fancied himself a ladies' man.

He wiggled his eyebrows. "Don't I always?"

Louise shook her head. "I'm glad my daughters are too old and my granddaughters too young. You behave yourself, young man."

Jimmy grinned. "Don't I always?"

With that he pulled open the door. But instead of walking out, he stopped and stared. His grin slipped. "Hey, that looks like...naw, it can't be."

"Who?" Rachel joined him, and so did Louise.

"Oh, my God." Louise gripped Rachel's arm so tight that her fingernails nearly broke the skin. "It's Harry."

Rachel frowned at the poor, battered dog stumbling and limping down the drive from the highway. The animal looked as though it had been dragged for miles over rugged ground. "It can't be." Harry had been in the plane with Dr. Ray and David. David never went anywhere without that dog. The poor fellow had been killed in the crash with them.

With a death grip still on Rachel's arm, Louise shoved past Jimmy and barreled out the door, dragging Rachel in her wake. "It's him, I tell you."

Jimmy, who also fancied himself a photographer, reached into his backpack for his camera, already seeing his photo credit and byline on the front page of the *Wyatt County Gazette*.

"Dad, look," Cody called. "It's a dog."

In the corral, Grady drew his mare to a halt and followed Cody's line of sight. He frowned. A stray dog. Unless things had changed a great deal while he'd been away, they didn't get many strays at Standing Elk. Everybody in three counties knew that Dr. Ray Lewis lived here. And if they knew that, they knew that Dr. Lewis would deliver a stinging lecture on the responsibility of pet ownership to anyone he caught dumping their unwanted animals out along the highway.

This dog had something wrong with it. It staggered

and limped badly. Its head hung low, and it appeared to be covered in dried mud. Maybe even blood.

And Cody was heading toward it.

"Cody." With visions of fangs and foaming mouths and rabid dogs dancing through his mind, Grady dismounted and vaulted over the corral fence. "Cody! Stay back," he cautioned, putting himself between Cody and the strange dog.

"No, Dad, look! It's Harry!"

Ah, hell, Grady thought. "Cody, you know it can't be, son."

"But it is!" Cody jumped up and down and would have taken off up the gravel road toward the pitiful-looking creature if Grady hadn't grabbed the back of his shirt as he darted around him. "Harry! C'mere, boy! Dad, let go. I know it's Harry."

Grady eyed the dog carefully and pulled Cody back.

When his dad and David had come to visit him and Cody in California, they had brought David's dog with them, because David refused to go anywhere without him, so both Grady and Cody were familiar with the dog. And this one did sort of resemble him. That might be all black hair under the dirt and whatever else covered it. That might be one white ear that gave the dog his distinctive, inquisitive look. But the dog had been in the plane with his dad and David on that fateful day. This couldn't be....

"Here, Harry, come here, boy!" Cody clapped and called and whistled, and the dog stumbled closer. Nothing more than hair and bones, poor fellow. Its tail tried to wag. "See, Dad? See? It's him!"

They never found the dog, Joe had told him. They

figured he had crawled off into the brush somewhere to die.

They never found the dog.

This poor dog was in such bad shape, Grady didn't see how he'd even made it down the drive from the road, much less from however far he'd come. But he whined so pitifully as he came near that Grady found himself holding out his hand for a halfhearted lick.

Those eyes. God, what a mix of pain and happiness.

The dog collapsed at Grady's feet.

Grady had been focused so intently on the dog and Cody that he hadn't paid attention to the trio approaching from the clinic until Rachel rushed forward and knelt in the gravel beside the dog.

"Harry. Oh, God, it is you, you poor thing. There, there, everything's going to be all right. You're home now, sweetheart."

"See, Dad? I told ya."

"I'll be d—" Remembering who he was talking to, Grady swallowed the swear word. "Well, I'll be."

Cody knelt on the dog's other side and looked like he was dying to reach out and pet him.

"Not yet, Cody," Rachel cautioned. "Let me see how badly he's hurt first. You don't want to touch some place that's sore and cause him more pain."

Grady watched as Rachel checked the dog over. The animal's face and feet were a mass of cuts and torn flesh, partially healed but still swollen and bloody. There was a long gash down his back right next to his spine, and what looked like a huge bite mark on one hip. Harry must have been to hell and back, more than once.

"How bad is he?" Grady asked Rachel.

"He's a walking miracle just for being here," she said softly. "But he's got infection in a dozen wounds or more, some of them pretty bad, most of them needing sutures. He's picked up enough parasites to choke an elephant. He's dehydrated, half-starved. I'd guess he's lost nearly a third of his weight. But the worst appears to be his right front leg."

"Is it broken?" Louise asked.

"Uh-huh," Rachel murmured. "And the shoulder is dislocated." She looked up at Jimmy, who hovered nearby, snapping pictures. "Stow that camera and go get the surgery ready."

Louise turned to go with Jimmy. "I'll go cancel this afternoon's appointments."

Rachel bit her lip. "I wish we had a stretcher."

Grady stepped forward and held out his arms. "Will I do?"

Rachel looked up at him as though she'd forgotten he was there. Doubt darkened her eyes.

Grady understood her misgivings. First, the poor fellow was hurting, and being picked up and carried in someone's arms would not be comfortable for him. And second, Harry was a fair-sized dog, his head reaching the middle of her thigh.

Grady knelt at the dog's back and, as gently as possible, slipped his arms beneath him, never mind the skin being scraped off the backs of his hands by the gravel beneath. "You said it yourself, Rach, he's lost a lot of weight."

Harry seemed to know that Grady wasn't hurting him intentionally. He whined once, but didn't struggle.

The four of them headed for the clinic—Rachel, Grady, Cody, and the dog who had miraculously found his way home.

For a minute, just a short span of time, Grady could have sworn he felt his brother at his side, urging him on.

Chapter Seven

It took hours to clean Harry up and put him back together. Jimmy stayed and helped Rachel and didn't care that his hot date might end up having to cool her heels.

Joe came looking for Grady and was astounded to learn about David's dog being alive and making it all the way home from the crash site. He rushed back to the house, and a few minutes later Alma came, with a jug of iced tea and a sack full of sandwiches.

Grady tried to get Cody to go back outside and play—even volunteered to go with him. But Cody was having none of it. Uncle David's dog was in that room behind that closed door, and Cody wasn't budging until he knew Harry was going to be all right. Not that he didn't trust his dad or Louise or Alma, but he wanted to hear it straight from Dr. Rachel. Nothing less would do.

Finally, rolling her shoulders to relieve an ache, Rachel emerged from the surgery, her face etched with lines of fatigue. Grady felt the strongest urge to go to her and hold her, rub those tired shoulders.

She wouldn't welcome his touch, so he'd just better get that idea right out of his head. That was what he told himself.

Cody jumped up from his chair. "Is Harry okay?"

Rachel smiled and brushed her hand across Cody's head. "He's still asleep right now, but I think he's going to be fine. It will take him some time to recover. He won't be able to go out and play for a few days yet, and when he does, he's going to be hobbling on three legs because one of them is in a cast. He'll need lots of rest, and lots of love."

Cody looked up at her, then at Grady. "Would it be all right if I loved him, Dad? Do you think he'd mind?"

God, what a good heart this kid had. "I don't think he'd mind at all, pard. In fact, it seems to me that Harry's your dog now."

Cody's eyes widened. "No foolin'?"

"No foolin'."

"You don't think Uncle David would mind?"

"I know he wouldn't. In fact, remember me telling you about a will, and how Grandad put in his will that he wanted you to have his ball cap and fishing tackle?"

"And the picture books."

"That's right. The photo albums," Grady said. "Your Uncle David had a will, too, and in it he said that if anything happened to him, he wanted you to have Harry."

If possible, Cody's eyes got bigger. "Golly. Really?"

"Uh-huh. That means you have to take care of him now. You have to feed him and make sure he always has clean water."

"And if he rolls in the manure, like he did when Uncle David brought him to see us that time, I have to give him a bath?"

"That's right. Do you think you can do all of that? It's a big responsibility, taking care of a dog."

"I can do it, Dad. Honest I can."

"I know you can, pard." Grady stood and stretched the kinks out of his back. "And now that we know he's going to be all right, we better get back to our chores."

"But, Dad," Cody protested. "I can't leave. I got reponsibilities here."

"Responsibilities," Grady corrected automatically.

"Yeah. I gotta look after Harry. He'll need me when he wakes up."

"He's not going to wake up for quite a while," Grady said. "Isn't that right, Rachel?"

"That's right." Rachel gave Cody a sober look. "He'll probably sleep clear through to tomorrow, seeing as he was so exhausted."

Over Cody's head, Grady mouthed a silent *thank you* to Rachel. He had visions of Cody wanting to spend the night curled up beside Harry in the cage Rachel had surely put him in after the surgery. He could envision it, because he'd done it himself once, when his own dog had been bitten by a rattler. He hadn't been much older than Cody at the time.

"So," Rachel continued, "you've got plenty of

time to get your chores done, eat supper, and get a good night's sleep before Harry will be ready for you to visit him.''

He could kiss that woman.

The thought startled him. Not because he'd had it. It was just an expression, after all. But because of the way the flippant notion softened and settled deep inside him. Making him think he really wanted to kiss her. Kiss her for real.

Speaking of real, you better get that way, pal. She doesn't want anything to do with you, and the feeling is mutual. Remember?

The trouble was, he suddenly found it hard to remember.

Jimmy got his photo credits and his byline. His pictures and article about the dog who survived a plane crash and, although severely injured, traveled more than a hundred miles home, made the front page of the next edition of the *Wyatt County Gazette*. Jimmy wasn't even too crushed when he realized that Harry, and not him, had become the talk of the town.

July Fourth dawned clear and warm. In Hope Springs anticipation filled the air, along with the clop of horses' hooves on pavement, the discordant notes of the high-school marching band tuning up, the shouts and laughter coming from the gathering crowd along Main as well as from the parade participants gathering at the north end of town, around the corner at the feed store.

Band members sweated under their wool uniforms. Majorettes twirled, dropped, retrieved, and tossed their batons in the air. Miss Wyatt County and Miss

Hope Springs were trying to see who could smile the widest, and they practiced their queenly waves as well as how to throw candy to the crowd without jostling their crowns. Horses stomped, snorted and fidgeted, as did their riders.

Every convertible in the county—all four of them—had been called into service and waxed to a mirror sheen, the better to show off the beauty queens, the mayor, and Bob Hodges, the state representative for the area. From their perches atop the back seats those dignitaries could wave, throw candy to the kids, and be seen well enough to get their pictures in the paper.

At the back of the line of parade participants the volunteer fire department lined up the hay wagon they would drive behind a six-mule team. Jefferson Polanski was giving his prized mules, on loan for the occasion, a last-minute grooming while they dozed in their traces.

Rachel looked around and smiled with pride. God, she loved this town, this county. She'd missed it terribly during the past seven years when she'd been away at school. But she was home now, and glad of it. This, she knew, was where she belonged. In Wyatt County among her friends and family.

If this was the year that Grady was to have ridden at her side as her husband, she refused to dwell on it. Refused to acknowledge the sudden blurring of her vision at the thought. She kept her smile firmly in place.

As she looked around at her family now, her smiled widened. They were an impressive bunch, the Wilders, even if she did say so herself. Especially when they were all dressed in jeans and matching red-white-and-blue shirts, white straw cowboy hats, and mounted on their favorite horses.

It was fun to watch the look on Belinda's face. This would be the woman's first year to ride with them, her first Independence Day as a Wilder. The first small-town parade she'd witnessed, let alone participated in.

Rachel nudged her horse closer to her sister-in-law's. "What do you think?"

"Think?" Belinda laughed. "I'm supposed to be able to think? The boys were up at four o'clock, insisting it was time to get ready. They're so excited, I keep expecting them to tear off down the street at a mad gallop."

Rachel pursed her lips to hold back a grin. "And of course, you're not excited at all."

"Who, me?" She gave an innocent blink with eyes that twinkled. "Okay, I admit it. This is fun."

"Yeah. After we—"

The shrill of a nearby whistle cut her off. It was time for the parade to begin.

The band, proudly sporting the Hope Springs High School banner, led the way. They got to go first so they wouldn't have to march through what the horses would leave on the pavement as they passed.

Rachel had bribed Ralph Sumner, the parade organizer, to let the Flying Ace entry—namely, the entire family plus the hands—follow the band. This way she would have time after they reached the other end of Main to race back via Pine Street and ride in the clinic's parade entry. The clinic's SUV would be pulling a decked-out trailer, as usual, but in the press of a busy week Rachel had neglected to get the details from Louise. The woman had merely told her to get her buns back to the trailer before it pulled out on Main near the end of the parade line.

The band turned the corner now and lined up on Main. Marching in place, they cut loose with a rousing rendition of "The Stars and Stripes Forever" and headed out.

Folks gathered along both sides of the street cheered.

Ace, beside Belinda at the head of the Flying Ace riders, turned in his saddle toward the rest of their group. "Are we ready?"

"Lead on, bro," Trey called.

"You boys ready?" Ace asked his sons.

"We *been* ready," Jason complained. "Let's *go,* Dad."

"All right." With a nod and a wink, he added, "Let's ride."

And they rode out in their matching shirts and hats at a respectful distance behind the marching band. Ace and Belinda took the lead and rode side by side. Behind them came their sons, Jason, Clay and Grant, trying their best to look solemn and dignified while breaking into giggles and waving at everyone they saw.

Behind the boys came Trey, Rachel and Jack, riding side by side, with Frank, Stoney and Donna, as the three highest-ranking Flying Ace employees, behind them, with the other hands bringing up the rear.

All in all, Rachel thought, a hell of a sight.

She held her breath while she smiled and waved, maintaining a close eye on the three little boys in front of her while also keeping a tight rein on her horse. There was always some joker in the crowd

who thought it was funny to toss out a firecracker
whenever anyone came by on horseback.

But this year, praise the Lord, the Wilder clan
made it the entire three-quarters of a mile down the
parade root to the end without incident.

Rachel waved goodbye to her family and trotted
her horse down the side street, then turned down Pine
and headed back toward the staging area. Toward the
clinic float. Toward...Grady.

"Are you sure about this?" Grady asked Louise
for the dozenth time that morning.

Louise rolled her eyes. "Will you *relax?* Every
kid in town is going to be envious of Cody for getting to ride in the parade."

"Yeah, and nobody can be meaner than a little kid
who's jealous," Grady said tersely.

"I didn't say *jealous,* I said *envious.* Nobody's
mean to the Wilder kids, or any other kids who get
to be in the parade. They're Wyatt County's version
of rock stars for the day. All those kids at the house
after the funeral will know who he is. They'll want
to be friends. It's perfect, I tell you."

"Is Daddy nervous?" Rachel asked.

Grady gave a start. He hadn't known Rachel had
arrived at the float until she spoke.

The float, as in years past, was a simple affair, a
flatbed trailer pulled behind the clinic's Mountaineer.
Bales of straw were stacked precisely to Louise's
specifications to provide perches for Rachel, Cody
and Harry.

If Louise had her way, Grady would be back there
on those bales, too, as he'd been when he was a boy
and he and David rode with their father. But Grady

had flatly refused. He might be a partner in the clinic, but he had nothing to do with its operations.

Louise, now, that was another matter entirely. She belonged on the float. She was the initial contact every person made when they called or visited the clinic. She was the one who finessed—sometimes co-erced—clients into paying their bills. She was the one who argued with suppliers and made sure med-icine and equipment was available to treat the ani-mals. She should be on the float.

Grady should not. He was firm about that.

But Cody…what a kick the kid was getting out of all of this. Grady was just worried that he could get hurt.

Oh, not physically. He wasn't likely to fall off the trailer or anything. But he didn't know any of those people who were out there now lining the street, waving and hollering at their friends. Would they wave and holler at Cody? Or would the clinic float pass by curious but silent onlookers?

The thought of Cody getting his feelings hurt was about to cripple Grady. "Yeah," he admitted to Ra-chel. He was nervous. "A little."

"Well, don't be." Rachel patted him on the arm on her way to straighten Harry's antlers.

Grady sucked in a quick breath. Such a casual touch, one that obviously meant nothing to her. To him, even though he knew better, it meant so much more. A hand on his arm, a gesture of…of what? Support? Encouragement? Friendship? Never had he thought to have even that much from her.

"Hold still, Harry," Rachel muttered, straighten-ing the papier-mâché antlers on the dog's head.

Harry gave her a sloppy doggy grin.

"You're eating this up, aren't you?" she asked him.

Harry's recovery was coming along nicely. His leg, which had required surgery to repair, was still in a cast, but he got around pretty well on the other three.

"Are we ready?" Cody danced beside Rachel and looked up at Grady. "Is it time? It's time, isn't it?"

Grady took in a deep breath and let it out slowly. "Yeah. It's time." He started to give Cody a boost up onto the bed of the trailer. He wanted to touch him, wrap his arms around him for just a minute during the lifting, to reassure himself that Cody would be fine, that he wouldn't get his feelings hurt out there on Main Street.

But Cody had already been up on the trailer and down a dozen times by himself and didn't wait.

Grady's arms felt empty. "Be careful," he cautioned as Cody jumped from one bale of straw to another. "You fall off, you're in trouble."

"Aw, gee, Dad," Cody said with disgust. "I don't fall off straw bales."

"Well, don't fall off the trailer." Grady turned away and saw Rachel starting to lift Harry in her arms.

"Here." He took the dog from her and put him up on the straw with Cody.

"Thanks." Rachel brushed her hands together, then gave him a big smile. "Now, one more."

Grady cocked his head. "You want me to lift you, too?"

"Nope." She nodded her head toward Louise, who was straightening the banner on the far side of the trailer. That banner read: Adopt a Pet from the

Animal Shelter. The one on the near side read: Spay/ Neuter Your Pets. Worm Your Stock. Vaccinate Everybody. They were Louise's pride and joy, and she wanted them to hang straight so everyone could read them. "Her," Rachel said.

Grady's smile was slow and wide. "You talked her into riding up there?"

"Nope. We're just going to ignore her and put her up there."

"Wilder," he said with a laugh, "I like your style."

"Well, then, Lewis, let's get to it."

Together they rounded the end of the trailer and each took one of Louise's arms.

"Hey, wha—?"

"Just come peacefully," Rachel told her as she and Grady dragged her toward the tail of the trailer, "and there won't be any need for rough stuff."

"No way, you two, I'm not—"

"Up you go." Grady grabbed her by the waist and lifted her onto the trailer.

"Grady Lewis—" She whirled and started to climb back down. "I'm not riding on this thing."

"Come on, Louise, you know you want to. You know Dr. Ray always wanted you to," Rachel added, thinking to play on Louise's emotions. She slipped into her white lab coat and tossed one each to Louise and Cody.

"And I'll tell you the same thing I told him every year," Louise said. "It's not my place. *He* was Standing Elk Clinic, and now *you* are." She pointed at Rachel. "I don't belong on display."

Grady didn't worry about playing on the woman's emotions. He pulled out the big guns. "I'm the ma-

Rachel and Cody. And Grady had to admit that he wasn't suffering any himself.

At the end of the parade route Grady pulled up and parked behind the giant stuffed moose on the Moose Lodge float and got out.

"Dad, Dad!" Cody leaped from one straw bale to another on his way to the back of the trailer, his oversized lab coat flapping in his wake and threatening to trip him. "Did you see, Dad, did you see? Wow! It was great!"

"I saw, I saw." Grinning, Grady held out his arms and Cody jumped. "Umph. You're almost too big for me to catch."

"Golly, Dad, I saw kids I knew and everything. It was way cool."

"Was it, now?"

Rachel sat on the end of the trailer and dangled her legs. "I hate to be the one to say I told you so," she said to Grady. She was grinning almost as widely as Cody was, and her eyes were filled with fun and laughter. "But—I told you so."

"Yeah." Grady glanced up at her, into those laughing blue eyes, and couldn't look away. "Yeah, you told me."

"Grandma, Grandma!" Louise's granddaughter rushed up, with Granddad in tow, and broke the spell. "You rided in the pawade!"

Before Grady could put Cody down and offer Rachel a hand, she scrambled down from the trailer on her own.

"Come on, pard," he told Cody as Louise's husband helped her down. "Let's go take this trailer and Harry home, then come back for some barbecue."

"Aw, Dad, does Harry have to go home?"

"As Harry's doctor," Rachel told him, "I think he's had about enough excitement for one day."

Grady knew Rachel was just trying to help him out. Harry was fully ready to spend the day in the park, hobbling around on three legs and letting every kid in sight pet him and feed him. But Grady wasn't prepared to keep an eye on him *and* Cody.

"But Cody can stay with me if he wants," Rachel added. "If it's okay with you. We've got a picnic spot staked out in the shade by the north parking lot, and the boys would love to spend the day with him. They ask about him all the time."

"Can I? Can I, Dad?"

"Let me think about it a minute." Grady turned to Louise. "I don't think Cody's met any of your grandkids, has he?"

"Mercy. I don't think he has," Louise claimed. "Come over here, Cody, and meet these kids." By now four more of her grandchildren had arrived.

As soon as Cody turned toward Louise, Grady faced Rachel. "What's your family going to say about Cody tagging along with you?"

Rachel blinked at him. "What are you talking about?"

"This is me, Rachel. I'm sure your brothers would just as soon not have anything to do with me or mine."

One corner of her mouth curved up. "Since when did you care what my brothers thought?"

"I don't want Cody getting caught in the middle."

If she'd been about to smile, now she was glaring. "You know better than that. My brothers are the most fair-minded men I know. They would never hurt a child, not for any reason."

Well, hell. She had him there.

"Besides," she said, her grin returning. "It will be a while before they make it to the park. Belinda volunteered them to clean up the street after the parade."

Now it was Grady's turn to blink. All his life the Wilder brothers, particularly Ace, as the oldest, had been bigger than life. The strong, macho type. A little intimidating, although, as Rachel had said, fair-minded. But the thought of those three rough, tough Wilder men—he couldn't help it. He broke out laughing.

"The great and mighty Ace Wilder is shoveling manure off Main Street?"

"So are Jack and Troy. I hope Belinda remembered the camera. Maybe Jimmy will get a picture for the paper."

"You've gotten mean over the years," Grady observed.

"Who, me?" She batted her eyes at him and fought a laugh. "It's just a little sisterly payback."

Grady gave in and let Cody go with Rachel and her nephews. It wasn't easy for him to stand back and watch Cody go off on his own, make friends on his own. But it was time, Grady knew, to let the boy take his own steps.

He and Joe took the dog and the trailer home. Then they hooked up the horse trailer and hauled their horses to the rodeo grounds. When he finally located Cody again, the kid was having the time of his life with the three youngest Wilders.

"Let him stay," Belinda said. "They're having a blast, and one more in this brood won't hurt a thing.

Or two, for that matter. You're welcome to hang out here if you want.''

Grady saw the way the Wilder men were eyeing him—with speculation, caution—and decided Cody was on his own. The boy had been accepted. Grady knew that acceptance on the part of Ace, Jack and Trey didn't extend to him.

Then there was Rachel, who was studiously ignoring him, now that they were off the float. Yep. Cody was on his own.

He thanked Belinda for the invitation but declined, then wandered away. It wouldn't be long before he would have to get back to the rodeo grounds, anyway.

The park was filled with people and booths. Food booths, craft booths and games of all kind. Grady grabbed a hamburger at one, a soft drink at another, and visited with some old friends who did seem glad to see him. Now and then Cody and his new Wilder friends dashed by with at least one adult Wilder in tow. Cody would yell at him and wave each time, and Grady was glad his son was accepted. Very glad indeed.

Rachel was having a ball running around the park with Belinda and the boys. They had to try all the games, visit with all their friends, sample all the food. This was not a day to worry about nutrition. Other than candy, they were allowed to eat and drink pretty much whatever they wanted.

But the soft-drink intake had its predictable results, so they herded the boys toward the cinder-block rest rooms at the edge of the park, where Belinda and Rachel took care of their own needs in the half marked Girls, then waited outside for the boys to emerge from the other side. They were still in there; they could hear them giggling.

Then it got quiet, but it was several more minutes before anyone came out. And then it wasn't the boys, it was Sheriff Martin.

"Ladies," he said with a nod. Then he walked briskly away across the grass and disappeared into the throng of people.

When the boys came out a moment later, they were wide-eyed and pale.

"Mom," Jason called, rushing to Belinda's side. "The sheriff called Cody a bad name and said he wasn't wanted around here and for him to find his daddy and go home."

Shocked, Belinda looked at Rachel.

Rachel stared at Jason, then Cody, then Jason. "He *what?*"

"He called Cody a bad—"

"Hush, son," Belinda said gently. "Aunt Rachel heard you."

Rachel knelt before Cody and studied his face. "Are you okay, honey?"

He was obviously upset, but he swallowed and nodded. "I'm okay. But do you know where my dad is?"

Rachel stood and pulled the boy to her side and wrapped her arm around him. "Not right this minute, but we'll find him, I promise."

They took the boys, much subdued now and confused, back to the family picnic spot.

"Keep them here," Rachel said.

"Are you going to find Grady?"

"In a minute. Right after I rip the hide off that no-good—"

Belinda held all four boys close to her and watched as Rachel spotted the sheriff in the crowd around one of the food booths and took off after him.

Grady finished off a second hamburger and wandered toward the Wilder picnic spot to see how Cody was doing. The minute he spotted him and the other boys, all four of them pale and huddled against Belinda, he knew something was wrong.

All his life Grady had heard the expression "seeing red," but until now he hadn't realized that it could be true. But as the boys excitedly repeated what had happened in the rest room, repeated the names the sheriff had called Cody, Grady's vision actually turned red. When he got his hands on that son of a bitch he was going to rip him to pieces, badge or no badge.

But first, there was Cody to see to.

Grady sat on the grass and pulled Cody down to his lap. It was a sign of how upset the boy was that he seemed to have forgotten he was too big to sit on a lap, especially in front of other people. But he not only sat there, he curled up against Grady's chest as if he never wanted to leave.

I'll kill him, Grady thought of the sheriff. *I'll flat-out kill him.*

"How come he said those things, Dad?"

Grady forced himself to take a deep breath for calm, and looked down at the most important person in his life. "You know how some animals are nice and some are mean?"

"Like that old bull back in California that used to kick everybody?"

"Yeah, like that. Some people are like that, too. Most are real nice, but some, well, they're not so nice. You just met one of the ones who's not so nice."

"But, Dad, he's the sheriff. I thought sheriffs were good guys."

"Well, they're supposed to be. And I imagine Sheriff Martin is usually nice, too, but he doesn't like me. Are you listening?" he asked when Cody started looking away.

"Uh-huh."

"It's me he doesn't like, Cody, not you. He was just taking it out on you because you were handy and I wasn't."

"That's not right."

"No, son, it's not right, and I'm real sorry he said those things to you. I guess he just figured if he could hurt your feelings, it was the same as hurting mine, and he was right about that."

"What's it mean, Dad?"

"What does what mean?"

"That word he called me. Bastard."

Oh, God, what was he supposed to say? He looked up to suddenly see all three Wilder men standing around Belinda and watching him.

"Go on," Jack said softly. "You're doing fine, Lewis."

Grady blew out a breath. How was he supposed to explain to Cody, while Jack, whose birth was also illegitimate, listened in?

"Well," he said finally. "It's got two meanings.

The real meaning is someone who's mom and dad never got married to each other.''

''You mean like you and my mother?''

''That's right.''

''But you said that's not so bad. How come he made it sound so bad?''

''I suspect it's because he really meant the word not so much for you, but for me.''

Cody's eyes widened. ''Golly. You mean Grandad never married Grandma, either?''

''No, Grandad and Grandma were married. When the sheriff used that word, he was using the other meaning that has nothing to do with whether or not a man's mom and dad were married.''

Interested now, with his color back to normal, Cody cocked his head. ''What's that?''

''Well, it means somebody you really hate, or you're really mad at. But when it's used like that, it's a bad word, a very bad word. Nobody should call somebody that, not ever.''

''How come the sheriff doesn't like you?''

The reasons were multitude, and most stemmed from Cody's birth, but Grady wasn't about to get into that. He still hadn't found a way to explain to Cody the sheriff was the boy's grandfather. After this incident, he was less eager than ever. There were other reasons, lesser reasons, that would make sense, though.

''Remember how Uncle David was, how he talked slow and didn't always understand things?''

''Yeah.''

''Well, when we were kids, we lived here, right there at our ranch, and we went to school here in town, where you'll go this fall.''

"So?"

"Not everybody understood Uncle David the way you and I do. Sometimes the kids at school would make fun of him and call him names."

"Did they call him a bastard?"

"No, and you're not to ever say that word again, you hear?"

"Golly, I was just askin', Dad." But there was a slight grin behind the protest that spoke of getting away with saying a bad word without worrying about getting called on it.

"Yeah, right." Grady pinched the tip of Cody's nose. "No, they called him a dummy."

Cody's eyes widened and lit with fire. "That's mean! That's not right. Uncle David wasn't no dummy."

"I know that, and you know that, but some of the other kids didn't understand."

"What'd you do?"

"Well, I did a bad thing. I picked fights with them. And the sheriff didn't like anybody getting into fights, no matter the reason. For that matter, Grandad didn't like it much, either."

"But Grandad never called you that word, did he?"

"No, because Grandad knew I wasn't just trying to be a troublemaker. But that's what the sheriff thought I was, so that's why he's never liked me."

Something new flitted across Cody's face. "This guy was the sheriff when you were a kid?"

"That's right. Sheriff Martin's been the sheriff around here for a long time."

"Golly. He sure must be old."

Grady chuckled, relieved that the crisis seemed to

be over. For Cody, at least. "Yeah, he's been around a while, but that's not something you should say. Some people are sensitive about their age. If you call them old, it could hurt their feelings or make them mad."

"Okay. But do we really have to go home, Dad? We was havin' fun."

"Who said we had to go home?"

"That man, that sheriff. He said I should have my daddy take me home, 'cause we wasn't wanted around here. That's not true, is it?"

"No, son, it's not true. Why, you've got three good friends right over there who don't want you to go home. Isn't that right, boys?" he asked the Wilder kids.

"Yeah, don't go, Cody," Jason said.

"Don't take him home, Mr. Lewis," Clay said. "Mom promised us ice cream if we didn't get sick by this afternoon. It's this afternoon, isn't it?" He craned his neck to look up at Belinda.

She pursed her lips. "Trust you to remember every little word. Yes, it's this afternoon."

"And us didn't get sick," said Grant, the three-year-old.

"Yeah," Jason said. "And a bargain's a bargain, right, Dad?" He looked up at Ace.

"Yep," Ace told his eldest. "And a woman's only as good as her word, so pay up, Mom."

"I want chocolate," Grant claimed.

Grady eased Cody off his lap, and the boy ran eagerly to his friends.

"Where's Aunt Rachel?" Jason wondered.

Grady had known she wasn't around, but now he,

too wondered. Especially when he saw the look on Belinda's face.

"She, uh, had to go talk to someone," Belinda said.

Grady rose slowly to his feet. "She didn't."

Belinda cast her gaze down at the boys, then nodded off toward the crowd in the park. "She did."

Grady felt the skin across his shoulders tighten. "She went after Martin?"

"With blood in her eye."

"Huh?" Jason asked. "What happened to her eye?"

"Nothing." Belinda herded the boys in the opposite direction to the one in which she had indicated Rachel had gone. "Let's go get that ice cream."

Cody and the boys went with Belinda. Grady tried to get Ace and his brothers to go, too, but they were having none of it.

"Rachel's our sister," Ace said flatly.

"Yeah," Trey said with relish. "And if she's takin' on the sheriff, I wanna watch."

"Dammit, Trey, it's not funny," Ace said.

"The sheriff isn't going to think so, that's for sure."

Chapter Eight

"Get outta my face, girl."

Rachel glared up at Sheriff Gene Martin with every ounce of outrage in her soul. He'd kept disappearing on her in the crowd, and it had taken her several minutes to snare the jerk. "You'll be begging me to do just that by the time I'm through with you. What the *devil* did you think you were doing, talking to that child that way?"

Martin snorted. "What child what way? I don't know what you're talking about."

"Maybe it's been a while since you've been around kids, if you think for a minute those four boys didn't come out of there repeating every word you said. Damn you, Sheriff. What you did was inexcusable."

"It's none of your business."

"It may be none of hers, but it's damn sure my business."

The sheriff sneered as Grady stepped up beside Rachel.

Grady poked his finger against Martin's chest. "If you ever go near that boy again, badge or no badge, I'm going to rip you to pieces. You got that, *Sheriff?*"

Martin's cheeks flushed. His nostrils flared. "Are you threatening an officer of the law?"

"No. I'm making a promise to a low-life jerk who picks on little children because it makes him feel like a big man."

The sheriff leaned into Grady. "Why, you little—"

"Afternoon, Sheriff Martin." Ace stepped up beside Grady and folded his arms. "Any trouble here?"

Rachel looked up to find not only Ace, but Jack and Trey as well, aligned with Grady. Her heart swelled with pride, with gratitude.

"I can't believe this," Martin blustered. "After the way this little sneak backstabbed your sister by running around with my LaVerne, you'd side with him?"

Grady motioned the Wilders back. "Whatever I did or didn't do to Rachel is between the two of us and nobody else. The same goes for me and LaVerne. That's your grandson you hurt today, Martin. Your own flesh and blood. Your daughter's flesh and blood. You might want to think about what you're cheating yourself out of by your attitude."

"And if that doesn't make you stop and think," Rachel said, not for a minute willing to take a back seat when the incident had occurred while Cody was in her care, "you might want to know that I'm the type of person who likes to write letters. Like, say, to the governor. Or the state attorney general. Letters about a county sheriff who likes to abuse little boys in the men's room."

Martin's face turned as red as a ripe tomato. "Why, you make it sound like—like—"

Rachel grinned slowly. "Yeah, I know. And not one word of it a lie. Try running for reelection with that hanging over your head. For that matter, try finishing out your current term."

"You'll pay for this." Martin glared at her, his cheeks vibrating with fury. "All of you." He turned and stomped off, knocking over a small table of soft drinks at the booth behind him in his haste.

Trey clapped Grady on the back. "Grady, my man, I think you've got yourself a serious enemy there."

Grady looked at Trey, then at Jack and Ace and Rachel. "So do you, since you seemed to think I couldn't handle the situation and decided to butt in. Not that I don't appreciate it," he told them, "but I don't see any sense in getting someone with that much authority mad at you when it's not your fight."

"My sons were there when he opened his big mouth," Ace said harshly. "I don't stand for anybody talking like that around my boys, and Cody's their friend. I don't stand for their friends being called ugly names, either. You got a problem with that, Lewis?"

Grady ran his tongue along his teeth and appreciated the fact that they were still there. Any minute he expected Ace to knock them loose. "Nope. Guess not."

As a group they turned and searched the crowd for Belinda and the boys, spotting them at the ice-cream booth twenty yards away.

"Come on." Trey nudged Grady and took Rachel by the arm. "Let's make Belinda buy."

Grady spent the next half hour making sure Cody was really all right. He had a bad moment once when he looked up and saw a uniform, but it was a county deputy rather than the sheriff.

Rachel called the man over and introduced him as Undersheriff Dane Powell. When Rachel made a point of introducing him to Cody, he realized what she was doing, and he wanted to kiss her right then and there. She was making sure that Cody wasn't left with the impression that all men wearing a uniform— particularly *that* uniform—were bad men. Powell was great with Cody, squatting down and spending several minutes talking easily with him and the Wilder kids.

Then, before Grady realized it, it was time to meet Joe at the horse trailer and loosen up the horses for their shot at the prize for team-roping.

Damn. He'd forgotten there would be events for little kids. Damn.

"What's wrong?" Joe asked.

"Look at that. They've got a calf pull for the kids. I should have got Cody in that."

"Yeah, and they'll have a stick-horse race, a greased-piglet chase, and a rooster grab."

"Damn. Maybe it's not too late. Maybe I can still get him in."

"Looks to me you're worrying for nothing. Look out yonder." Joe used his chin to point to the arena.

It was a good thing that Gray Ghost was a patient horse, because it was another forty-five minutes before Grady made it back to finish saddling her. That was how long he spent watching Cody and a couple of dozen other kids under the age of ten run up and down the length of the arena in one event after another, laughing, shrieking, falling down only to get up and laugh and run again.

Five minutes into the first event—the calf pull, where a dozen calves, each with a prize ribbon tied onto its tail, tried to keep out of the reach of the screaming, laughing children who would try to grab a ribbon—someone nudged his elbow where he stood at the arena fence.

"Move over." It was Rachel, with her face behind a camera. "We need pictures."

"Was this your idea, letting Cody take part with your nephews?"

"Nope, it was theirs. We figured it would take his mind off what happened earlier."

"Thanks, Rach."

She smiled at him. "You're welcome. He seems fine, by the way."

"Yeah. Good." He reached for his wallet. "There had to be entry fees. Plus all that food and ice cream you've been treating him to. What do I owe you?"

She narrowed her eyes and shot him a glare. "Don't insult me, Lewis. Besides, you're going to need your money. I heard them planning a sleepover at your house for the near future."

She snapped three pictures before the people in the front row of the stands behind them complained they were blocking the view.

"Come on." Rachel grabbed Grady's hand and

started up the steps of the old wooden bleachers. "We've got great seats. I can use the zoom."

Grady had a dizzying sense of falling down a tunnel and coming out as a teenager. How many times had he and Rachel run up and down these steps over the years to find his family or hers, or climb all the way to the top to sit together, just the two of them? Too many times to count.

Her entire family was there now. Ace stood in the aisle with a video camera aimed at the action in the arena. Below the camera, his grin was wide.

All four of the boys managed to snag a ribbon from the tail of a calf. None of them won the stick-horse race—three girls beat them. A kid from town finally caught the greased pig, thank goodness. Grady didn't know what they'd have done with a pig if Cody had caught it. And one of Louise's grandsons caught the rooster.

Through it all Grady forgot that he was surrounded by Wilders, most of whom probably still had it in for him. He was too busy laughing, and so were they, to worry about anything else at the moment. They laughed so hard, all of them, they had tears streaming down their faces, Grady included.

"Oh, God." Jack used the palms of his hands to wipe the tears from his face. "Ace, I hope you got that. That's blackmail material for sure."

But Ace couldn't answer. He and Belinda were hanging on to each other and still laughing too hard to speak.

"Let's get outta here," Trey said, nudging Jack. "We've got horses to see to. I'm not letting Lewis here collect the prize money for team-roping 'cause you were laughing too hard to get the job done."

"Me?" Jack protested. "You weren't laughing your fool head off at all. And Lewis and Helms aren't taking that prize, we are. See you later, Grady. We'll be the ones with the fastest time."

"In your dreams, Wilder," Grady called as Jack and Trey started down the bleachers.

"See?" Rachel said. "I told you you didn't have anything to worry about where my brothers were concerned."

Grady shrugged. Maybe he'd been worried for nothing, but he still couldn't see the Wilders letting him off the hook for what they all thought he'd done to Rachel in the past.

"Thanks, by the way," he told her, "for having Cody down there with the others."

"Ha. We couldn't have kept him away, not when Jason decided they were all going to enter."

"Well, thanks anyway. I forgot they were having kid events, or I'd have been here to see that he entered."

"Dad! Dad!" four young voices called as the boys clamored up the bleachers. Three were addressing Ace. But Cody saw Grady and ran straight for him, grinning like a loon. "I won a ribbon! Did you see? Did you, huh?"

"I saw, I saw." Grady scooped the boy up and gave him a bear hug, then put him down quickly so as not to embarrass him. He was, after all, five years old, no longer a baby, according to him. "I'm just glad you didn't get your hands on that greased pig."

"Aw, heck, Dad, I wanted that pig."

"Yeah," Clay hollered. "We wanted that pig. Can we have a pig, Dad?" he asked Ace.

"Sure," Ace told him. "Think of all that free bacon we'd have."

"Aw, Dad."

Grady and Joe won the team-roping. They beat the next best time—Trey and Jack's—by four-tenths of a second. Rachel had a bad moment when she spotted Grady getting ready to swing up into the saddle shortly before the event.

It was a simple thing, really. He reached up and stroked his mare's glossy gray neck. That's all it took to plunge her deep into remembering how that same hand felt stroking her own neck. Her shoulders, her arms. Her breasts.

She caught herself closing her eyes while sitting there in the stands and letting the remembered touch of his callused palm and those clever fingers bring her pleasure enough to make her blood race, then, and now.

With a shudder, she popped her eyes open in shock.

"Are you cold?"

Rachel blinked and turned her head slowly toward Belinda, seated next to her. "What?"

"You shivered. I asked if you were cold."

Heat swept up her cheeks. "Uh, just a little."

"There's a jacket or two in the Suburban," Belinda offered.

Rachel swallowed. "Thanks, but I'm fine. Really."

This wouldn't do. Hadn't she told herself over and over that she had to put the past behind her? How was she to do that when her own mind—even her body—betrayed her at every turn?

Well, no more, she decided. This was the nation's Independence Day, and it would become hers, too.

Ace had gone down to the chutes with Jack and Trey to give them some last-minute advice on their roping. As soon as he returned to the stands and Rachel could get away without leaving Belinda alone with four boys, she made her escape.

She'd been working too hard, that was all. Seven straight years of college—most of it twelve months a year—then home to start work immediately, then Dr. Ray and David's deaths. Then Grady's return.

She'd been seeing too much of him in and around the clinic. She needed to spend some casual time with other people, that was all. Take some time for herself. So she wandered the park in the late afternoon and caught up with a number of old friends whose friendships she had, of necessity, neglected since high school. She met spouses and children she'd only heard about in passing, and it felt good to reconnect with familiar people from her childhood and teen years in a new, adult way and to meet their families.

When a little voice in the back of her mind whispered that all her old friends were married and had children, and that time was passing her by, she moved from group to group faster to flee it, laughed a little louder to drown it out.

She found her family again in time to share the barbecue dinner for which the Flying Ace had supplied a whole steer.

It wasn't quite sunset when the country band, hired from Laramie, started tuning up for the street dance. The city had blocked off the park's north parking lot, just a few yards from the Wilders' picnic spot, for the night's dance.

Before heading that way Rachel noticed Trey's cup was only half full of beer. She snagged it when he wasn't looking and took it with her. But she didn't go straight to the improvised dance floor. Instead, she spent the first few songs wandering around again, saying hello, watching small children fall asleep in their suppers from playing so hard all day long.

On her way back toward the parking-lot-cum-dance-floor, she paused at a trash can, drained the last swallow of beer from her cup, and tossed the cup in.

Now, she thought, dusting off her hands and heading for the music. *Who's the best dancer in town?*

The band was between songs and Grady was talking to Danny Warden when a sudden tingling swept down his spine.

Rachel.

Somehow, he knew she was there behind him. He could feel her, sense her, just like in the old days, and it shook him. He didn't want to be that aware of her.

He saw Danny's gaze stray, his eyes widen. "Hi, Rachel. Hey," he said, his gaze darting from Rachel to Grady. "Are you two back together? Man, that's—"

"No," Rachel and Grady said together.

Danny blinked. "Oh. Uh, well, whatever you say." He was grinning like a chicken-eating possum. "I see my wife flagging me down. I'll just be running along now so the two of you can, uh, not be together."

Slowly, so as not to aggravate the knee he'd wrenched during the team roping event, Grady turned to face her.

With her hands planted on her hips, Rachel smirked at Danny's hasty retreat.

Grady couldn't help but take the time to notice that nobody, man, nobody filled out a tight pair of jeans better than Rachel Wilder. Most of the time since he'd been back she'd worn her clothes more loosely, or had on that white lab coat that covered her to her knees. But not tonight. He'd been trying not to notice all day, but now he let himself look.

"What are you staring at?" she demanded.

"Uh, nice…boots."

Her face brightened. "You like them?" She stuck one foot out and turned it this way and that, showing off a pair of hand-tooled goatskin boots that looked as if they'd cost a month's pay.

"Yeah," he said. "Nice."

"Thank you." The band started up again with a rousing country two-step. "Do you still remember how to dance?" she asked over the blare of guitars blasting from the huge speakers.

"Is that your way of asking me to dance?" he asked back, surprised.

"No, it's my way of asking if you remember how."

Chagrined, feeling as if he'd been tricked—which he had—he said, "Yeah, I remember how."

"Good. *This* is my way of asking you to dance." She snared him by the arm and started toward the mix of couples two-stepping around the edges of the parking lot.

It was nearly impossible to hold a woman close

during a fast-paced two-step—especially when he was trying to baby his bad knee—but the dance did give Grady the right to hold her hand with one of his and place the other at her waist. At least, that's the way it was supposed to go.

But Rachel obviously had other ideas and looped her arms around his neck. "Now," she said, leaning closer than was practical for the dance. "Do you want to dance with me, Grady?"

He ran his tongue along the inside of his cheek. "Yeah, I guess so."

"Good. I'm celebrating," she said emphatically.

Something wasn't quite right here, Grady realized. Her smile was too smug, her eyes just a little glazed, and her breath hinted of something other than barbecue. "You're plowed."

She reared back and missed a step. "I am not."

Grady threw back his head and laughed. "Oh, yes you are. You never could hold an ounce of liquor. You're drunk as a skunk."

"I only had half a cup of beer."

"Rach, a half a cup of beer used to be enough to knock you on your sweet little rear."

Her fingers crept up into his hair. "You think my rear's sweet?"

"You are definitely wasted."

"I'm not wasted. I told you, I'm celebrating."

"What are you celebrating?"

"It's Independence Day."

"That's right. July Fourth."

"No, *my* Independence Day." Clasping her fingers together behind his neck, she leaned back so that he carried her weight. "I'm celebrating my independence from you, Grady Lewis."

Maybe she had the right idea in getting drunk. He could use a beer, or something stronger, himself. "You've been independent of me for a long time, Rach. Five years, in fact."

"Nope." She shook her head so hard that if he hadn't had a good hold on her, she would have fallen. "I thought so, too, but s'not true."

"S'not?"

"No, s'not, snot."

The old joke should have made him laugh. Instead it made him ache.

"But s'gonna be. I'm gonna be independent of you. From now on."

Grady kept his mouth shut and went on dancing her around the lot. There wasn't much he could say to a statement like that, and he figured the less he said, the less she'd have to get mad about tomorrow when—if—she remembered this conversation.

Hell. Half a beer.

"Oh, Grady." She stopped dancing and pressed herself full against his chest. "I don't wanna be independent from you."

Before his feet stopped along with his heart and they got trampled by the other dancers, Grady wrapped both arms around her waist and, staggering slightly because of his knee, carried her onto the sidewalk and out of the dancing.

"Come on, honey, let's get you back to your family so they can take you home." He knew she was going to regret this, big time, come tomorrow.

They must have looked like two drunks, instead of a sober man trying to help a tipsy woman, he thought wryly as they staggered across the grass together—she impaired by an ounce of beer, he by his bum knee. His rodeo days, he feared, were over, thanks to that knee.

It wasn't quite dark yet when they neared the Wilders' picnic site, but the three oldest kids, which included Cody, were sprawled on a blanket, dead to the world. The youngest slept soundly in Ace's arms.

But having his son asleep in his arms didn't prevent Ace from snarling at Grady. "Dammit, Lewis, look at her. She's drunk."

"Don't I know it. Somebody give me a hand, will you?"

Rachel beamed at her brothers. "Oh, he doesn't need a hand. He's got two very nice ones of his own."

"This is low, Lewis," Jack told him coldly, "even for you."

"What?" Grady protested. "I didn't—"

"You didn't get her drunk so you could take advantage of her?" Trey demanded.

Grady rolled his eyes as he struggled to get Rachel to the folding chaise lounge beside the tree. "Great. This afternoon you were taking up for me, now you're ready to kick my teeth in."

As Ace passed the sleeping Grant to his wife, he growled, "It's not your teeth you're going to lose, Lewis."

Rachel fell onto the chaise lounge and giggled. "Silly brothers. Why would he want to take advantage of me? I'm the one he walked out on, remember?"

Trey glared at Grady. "Oh, we remember, all right. So she's still not good enough for you, is that it?"

Belinda watched, startled, as her husband and

brothers moved in on Grady. "Idiots," she hissed. "First you're mad because you think he's taking advantage of her, now you're mad because he's not. Here." She thrust Grant into Grady's arms and shoved him toward the chaise next to Rachel's. "Sit."

"Yes, ma'am." Grady never argued with a woman with that particular look in her eye.

"What are you doing?" Ace demanded.

She hissed in irritation. "You can't hit him when he's holding your son."

Grady was just fond enough of his teeth—and whatever other parts they were threatening—to appreciate the wisdom, and the humor, in her reasoning. He sat

"He doesn't need to hold my son."

"Need I remind you that the sheriff would just love an excuse to haul all of your sorry rears to the county jail? A nice friendly fight in front of all these witnesses would be just the excuse he's looking for. Now, back off," she snarled to her husband and his brothers.

"Yes, ma'am," they muttered.

"Now, you—" She jabbed Ace in the chest with a forefinger. "Help me get Rachel home and put to bed."

Grady glanced over at Rachel to see how she was taking all of this. She was out cold.

Chapter Nine

It was pitiful the way a half cup of beer could do such damage to the human mind and body. First the embarrassment of getting drunk, then the pain and humiliation of the hangover the next morning. Rachel had showered, then downed three cups of coffee before she dared to look at herself in a mirror.

She should have made it four cups. Not that the extra caffeine would have helped the bags under her eyes, but maybe it would have cleared her vision enough so she could appreciate them more fully.

She couldn't believe she'd forgotten that she had no tolerance for alcohol. None. Zero. How could she have forgotten?

And how, she wondered frantically, had she gotten home? Her car was in the driveway, but she hadn't driven it yesterday. Had she walked? Had someone brought her? Grady? It was all so fuzzy.

Had she undressed herself and put herself to bed? She seemed to recall…no, she seemed to recall having help getting undressed!

Grady was in the tack room in the barn when he heard a car pull up out on the gravel drive. It was Sunday, barely noon; he wasn't expecting anyone, so he stayed put.

Not that he had much choice in the matter. Damned knee. Gingerly he shifted his weight and leaned against the table to peer around the open door.

Ah, hell. What was Rachel doing here? He wasn't ready to see her again after last night at the park.

But ready or not, here she came. Like a bloodhound, she'd sniffed out his lair and made straight for the tack room.

"Hi."

The dark glasses couldn't hide the pallor of her skin. "Hi, yourself. How are you feeling?"

She swallowed. "Like the entire parade ran over me. I, uh, I'd like to apologize."

Grady kept his hands busy rubbing saddle soap into an old set of reins. "For what?"

"For…for whatever I did last night."

He smirked. "Don't remember, do you?"

"It's…a little fuzzy. I think we danced?"

"We danced."

"Is there…anything else I need to apologize for?"

"My virtue's still intact, if that's what you're worried about. Take off those glasses."

"Oh, uh, no, that's all right."

"Coward."

"All right, but it's not a pretty sight." She slipped off the dark glasses.

Grady let out a low whistle. "Nice set of Samson-ite you've got hanging there."

"Samsonite?"

"Bags, Rach. You've got bags under your eyes. And the whites are full of interesting little red lines. Like a road map of Georgia."

Her jaw flexed in irritation. "Thank you. I hadn't noticed."

Grady kept working. A silence built, and not a comfortable one. He finally broke it. "You really don't remember asking me to dance last night?"

"I asked you?"

"Well, not really. You dragged me out into the thick of things and said you wanted to dance. Said a few other things, too."

"Dare I ask what?"

He put the reins down and turned toward her.

He shouldn't have. The incautious movement sent shards of agony stabbing through his knee, and from there, down to his foot and up to his hip. Red spots of pain danced before his eyes.

"Grady!" Rachel was at his side in an instant, placing her shoulder beneath his arm to support him.

"I'm all right," he managed after a hiss of pain.

"Like hell you are. What is it, your foot? Your knee? Hold on." With the toe of her sneaker she caught the leg of a tall wooden stool and dragged it closer. "Sit down."

He didn't have the breath to argue.

"You idiot. Look at that knee. Your jeans are so tight around it, it's a wonder you got them on at all."

"It wasn't that bad when I got dressed."

"What did you do to it?" She probed gently and set his teeth on edge.

"Easy," he barked.

"Don't be a baby." She knelt before him and put her palm to the knee. "If you can walk around on it, I can touch it. It's hot, and about three times its normal size. You need to pack it in ice."

"You're only licensed to work on animals," he said tersely.

"That's right. And right now I'm checking out a stubborn mule. Or a jackass, maybe. You banged it up good yesterday, didn't you?"

"I guess."

"And before that?"

"Some. Stop fussing, will you?" he said irritably.

She looked up at him. "Somebody needs to fuss over you. You must have hidden this pretty good from Alma. She wouldn't have let you out of the house on a knee like this."

"She's not my keeper, and neither are you."

"I'm going to assume it's the pain that's making you testy."

"Hmph. You're what's making me testy. I'm getting tired of being jerked around."

She pushed herself to her feet and balled her fists at her waist. "You want to explain that remark, buster?"

"You know what I'm talking about." He eased himself more fully onto the stool. He'd be damned if he'd give her the satisfaction of seeing him fall on his butt. "Ever since I've been back you've been jerking me around."

"I have not," she protested.

"First you want to be friends, then you don't. Then you want your independence from me, whatever the hell that means, then you don't. Just what *do* you want from me, Rachel?''

She stared at him blankly for a moment, then lowered her hands to her sides and relaxed her fists. ''I want you to kiss me.''

Stunned, shocked, Grady gaped. ''You want *what?''*

She gave him a fleeting smile. ''I guess that's my answer, huh?'' She turned toward the door.

''Rachel, wait.'' He lunged to his feet and reached for her. His knee gave again, and again, she caught him.

But he caught her, too. Caught her, wrapped his arms around her, and held her close. Maybe, he thought, if he obliged her, if he kissed her, he could get her out of his head once and for all. The mind had a way of remembering things better than they really were. The reality of kissing Rachel couldn't be nearly as staggering as his memories.

An instant later, when his mouth settled on hers, he knew he'd been wrong. On both counts. Kissing Rachel was even more staggering than he'd remembered. And it wasn't about to get her out of his head. Not now, not ever, he realized as he sank into the kiss and drank in her welcoming response.

Wants and needs bubbled up from the deepest part of him and became part of the kiss. With one hand, he cupped her head. With the other, he relearned the feel of her, the shape, every curve and dip, every swell of muscle that he could reach.

It wasn't enough. Would never be enough. And it was the biggest mistake of his life, kissing her. He knew that even as he demanded more from her. She gave it and demanded her own share back.

He wanted more. More than this single kiss. He wanted all of her. Things he'd never had from her before.

But this was Rachel, the woman who thought he'd betrayed her. The woman who hadn't trusted him enough to let him explain.

"No," she moaned when he pulled back and ended the kiss. "Don't stop."

His chest was heaving. He couldn't catch his breath.

She didn't want to stop? Even believing what she did about him? She humbled him. Unnerved him. "I don't want to stop," he admitted. He devoured her mouth again and felt the need build, tasted an answering need in her. His hands turned greedy, his blood hot. "I don't want to stop with just a kiss."

"Want me," she breathed, peppering his face with kisses. "Want me, Grady."

"You know I do." He took her face in both hands and looked at her, read the acceptance in her eyes. Acceptance of him, of the past, everything. And he read the offer, as well. She was offering him everything. Paradise. "I always wanted…"

"Wanted what?"

"Too much, I guess," he confessed, shaking his head. "I always wanted to be your first."

Her eyes lit, her lips curved. "Just let me shut this door, and you will be."

Grady's heart skipped one whole beat. Then another. She couldn't mean… "What did you say?"

"Don't look so stricken. It means I'm a virgin, not a leper." Her laughter sounded of nerves. "Is that a problem?"

Yeah, he thought. It was. "You…never?"

One corner of her mouth moved into a wry smile. "What did you think, that you'd leave town and I'd hop into bed with the next guy that came along? After telling you no all my life?"

"But...five years?"

She shrugged. "Is that a problem?" she asked again. The shrug shifted her breasts against his chest and had him closing his eyes in reaction.

Twenty-six years old, and still a virgin. The knowledge staggered him. He was torn between wanting to scoop her up in his arms and carry her, if not to a real bed, to the musty old cot in the corner, or running scared in the opposite direction as fast as he could go.

Scared, because if the offer of her virginity meant she still cared for him, the ramifications were staggering. Scared, because she needed protection—from him. From this overwhelming urge inside him to drag her off by her hair, like some caveman.

He couldn't think. Didn't know what to do, what to say. She hadn't trusted him enough five years ago to listen to his explanation of what had happened, but now she offered herself to him? It made no sense. In any case, he had no business accepting that offer and taking what he wanted from her without first telling her the truth. She thought she was giving herself to a man who had betrayed her.

"I don't know what to say," he told her.

The light in her eyes dimmed. "Well, then I guess you've said it, haven't you?" She pulled away from him, her cheeks a bright, flaming red.

"Rachel, no. I didn't mean—"

She turned toward the door.

"Dammit, Rachel, don't—" He had taken a step

toward her, but his knee gave out. He barely caught himself on the work table before suffering the indignity of crashing to the floor.

"I'd get that knee looked at if I were you," she said over her shoulder in a choked voice as she walked away.

Jaw clenched in pain—from his knee, from her—Grady watched her leave. Damn her. She still wasn't going to let him explain anything.

Rachel crammed her sunglasses back on to hide the tears threatening to blind her and took the last few steps to her car at a run. Once inside, she floored the accelerator and flung gravel behind her all the way until she hit the highway and pavement.

Stupid, stupid, stupid. How could she have been so stupid as to have asked him to kiss her?

And why, when he obliged her, was it even more earth-shattering than she had remembered?

The tears gathering in her eyes spilled down onto her cheeks. She left them there and gripped the steering wheel, concentrating on keeping her speed down to a reasonable—legal—level, when what she really wanted to do was curl up in a tight ball and give in to the pain eating at her heart. Five years ago he'd rejected her by fooling around with LaVerne Martin behind her back. Today he had just flat-out rejected her.

When are you going to learn, Rachel?

But what was she supposed to learn? That she wasn't over him, had never gotten over him? Or was she perhaps supposed to realize, once and for all, that she wasn't and never had been as important to him as he was to her?

"No." She refused to taint all those years of memories by believing that their past had never meant anything to Grady. He *had* loved her. She couldn't be wrong about that.

At the city limits she slowed down even more and drove straight through town without even thinking about turning off on her street. She headed south down the county highway to the place she always went when she hurt, like a wounded animal to its lair. To the Flying Ace.

But all the way there, she kept seeing the look that had seeped into Grady's eyes when he realized she had never been with a man. It had looked suspiciously like...fear.

At the realization, her tears dried up as if someone had turned off a faucet.

What, precisely, had he been afraid of?

From the time she was ten, when her parents died, Rachel had always taken her troubles to Ace, who was ten years older than she and, after their parents' deaths, head of the family. There wasn't anything should couldn't talk to Ace about. He'd been the one to tell her about boys, about sex. He'd been the one whose shoulder she'd cried the hardest on when Grady left. She could talk to Jack, too; he was a good listener. But mostly she had talked to Ace.

Yet after the regular Sunday dinner, after the cleanup, when it was nearly time for her to head back to town, Rachel found herself seeking out Trey. Because he was only two years her senior, they had a different relationship, in many ways closer than her relationships with Ace and Jack. Plus, he was only a year older than Grady, and he knew Grady better than their older brothers did.

She found Trey standing in the kitchen tossing his car keys in the air, getting ready to head for his house on the other side of the ranch. She snagged his keys out of the air and threaded her arm around his.

"Take a walk with me before you leave," she said.

He studied her a minute, then nodded. "Okay."

Arm in arm they strolled down the road toward the barn and corrals.

"What's on your mind?" he asked.

Rachel was grateful that he'd decided not to bring up her drinking and subsequent hangover again. She'd already taken enough flak from the family about that. Sheesh. A girl drinks half a beer, gets a little tipsy, and has to put up with stupid jokes and wisecracks all day.

"It wouldn't be Grady, would it?" Trey asked.

Rachel smiled slightly. "What makes you think that?"

"I don't know." He gave a casual shrug. "Seemed like you two were making a little progress yesterday, until you drank yourself into a stupor."

She rolled her eyes in disgust. "I did not drink myself into a stupor. It was your fault, anyway. It was your cup I swiped."

"I wondered what had happened to it. Hell, kid, there wasn't enough beer left in that cup to drown a flea."

"This is *not* what I wanted to talk to you about."

"What, then?"

Okay. She had his attention. Now how was she supposed to broach the subject?

"Must be pretty serious," Trey observed.

This time it was Rachel who shrugged. "Not really. It's just... I've got a hypothetical question for you."

"Hypothetical?"

"Yes. It's, well, it's about men. I need to get inside a man's—a hypothetical man's—head."

"Uh-huh. Okay. Shoot. Metaphorically, that is."

She didn't know any way to do this other than to simply jump in. "Why would a man get scared when a woman he says he wants tells him she's...never been with a man before?"

Trey choked.

Rachel rolled her eyes and slapped him on the back, two hard whacks.

"Okay, okay! You're killing me. Jeez Louise, Sis."

"Well," she said, folding her arms across her chest and looking out to the rangeland beyond the corrals. "I guess that confirms that it's not just hypothetical men who are afraid of even the word *virgin*."

"Are you—"

"I was speaking hypothetically. I believe I made that perfectly clear."

"Uh, yeah. Hypothetically. Right."

"So what is it?" she cried throwing her hands in the air. "Is a man afraid a virgin won't know how to do it?"

"Ah, jeez, why are you asking me?"

She shot him a narrow-eyed glare. "I suppose I could go find a street corner to stand on and ask the first man who comes along. If a girl can't ask her own brother these things, who's she supposed to ask?''

''You could ask Ace, or Jack. Or Belinda. Yeah, you could ask Belinda.''

''I'm asking you.''

''All right, all right. It's just that I don't…well, hell, I don't know. I don't have any experience with that type of woman.''

''You've never…with a virgin? Why not?''

''Because I don't know any nuns, all right?''

''Oh, that's just too cute, Number Three. Now you're calling me a nun.''

''Oh, really? I thought we were speaking hypothetically.''

''I'm not ashamed to admit I've never slept with a man.''

''And you shouldn't be,'' Trey said, suddenly serious. ''Sex isn't…it isn't a thing to be taken lightly. It's serious business. A woman ought to be damned picky about it, if you ask me.''

''And a man?''

''A man, too.''

''What about this hypothetical man?'' she asked, bringing Trey back to the subject she couldn't let go of. ''Why would he get upset and scared just because a woman hadn't…you know.''

''Jeez, you're asking me all these questions and you can't even say it? Just because she hadn't had her oil checked.''

It was nerves, she decided, that made her laugh. ''Trey.''

''It's intimidating, all right?''

''What's intimidating? The word *sex?*''

''No, the thought of having sex—and it shouldn't

be *having sex.* If it's a woman's first time, it should be *making love,* not just sex.''

''Why is it intimidating?''

''Well, hell, a guy would start wondering if he knew how to make sure she enjoyed it. The first time for a woman can be…''

''Painful?''

He shrugged. ''So I'm told. A guy would want to make sure he didn't, you know, hurt her or anything. Or scare her. He'd be worried that he'd do something she didn't like and make her not ever want to be with a man again.''

Rachel stared off into the distance again, at the mountains this time, and sighed. The sun was slipping behind the peaks. ''Okay. I guess I can see that.''

In a nearby pasture a calf bawled for its mother. The mother gave an answering moo.

Trey's lips twitched. ''So you scared him, huh?''

Rachel pursed her lips and refused to answer.

''I knew Grady wasn't dumb.''

''Who said anything about Grady?''

''Oh, right. This is some hypothetical guy we're talking about. A smart one, too. Smart enough to step back and think before he does something they might both be sorry for. If he was somebody like Grady, and she was somebody who maybe had reason to think he might hurt her again, well, that would really make him stop and think. He'd have to wonder why she would even let him near her. And if he was any kind of a man, he'd want to make damn sure he knew what he was getting into, because he would never want to hurt her again. He might even be thinking she might be better off without him.''

The peaks swallowed the last of the sun.

Was that it? Rachel wondered. Was that what Grady had been thinking? She wasn't sure, and wouldn't know unless she asked him, and even then he might not tell her.

She appreciated Trey more than she could say. Family. They were always there for her. She didn't know what she would do without her brothers, and now Belinda.

How had Grady stood being away from his family for so long? Away from everything familiar to him. Alone, except for Cody. Except for whatever new friends he made, whatever comfort he might have found.

She remembered when he first came home a few weeks ago, how the pain of his past betrayal had risen up and nearly strangled her. It still hurt to think about it, but the pain was different. Less. It was more a pain for all they'd lost, everything that had been denied them. Yes, he had hurt her. But even more, he had hurt *them*. He had robbed them of their future together.

Well, he was back now. The future was still out there. And she still wanted it, that future with Grady. Incredible as it seemed in light of what he'd done, she still wanted him.

He might very well break her heart again. He might not return these feelings that were bubbling to life inside her. And even if he did, she might never be able to trust him again, even if he wanted her to.

But Grady was so handsome, so masculine. He was smart and clever and fun to be with. He had a ranch of his own and an adorable son. How long was he going to want to live alone? How long before he decided it was time to share his life with a woman?

If Rachel didn't take a chance on him now, she might never have another opportunity. She couldn't imagine her first lover being anyone but Grady. He was the only man she'd ever loved. If he broke her heart again, well, she'd survived that pain once, she could survive it twice.

"What are you going to do?" Trey asked her quietly.

Slowly she smiled and turned to her brother. "What do you think I'm going to do?"

A smile spread across Trey's face. "Should I warn him?"

"You can if you want, but it won't do him any good. The man is a goner, or my name's not Rachel Wilder."

Chapter Ten

This whole thing would have been easier if she had the slightest idea how to go about seducing a man, but she figured there had to be some truth to that old adage that the way to a man's heart was through his stomach.

If she was going to do this, she needed something to make him weak. Something to make him beg. So Monday at noon she zipped into town and paid a visit to Sumner's Drug Store and picked up one of Ida's peach cobblers—an entire cobbler—to go. When a woman was this serious, she wanted the most potent ammunition available.

She stashed it in the refrigerator at the clinic and waited until the end of the day, when she urged Louise out the door.

"Aren't you leaving?"

"In a little while. I want to look through those

résumés we've been getting.'' They'd placed an ad
for another vet and had received three responses so
far. Swearing she wouldn't stay long, she waved
goodbye and sent Louise on her way.

As soon as Louise was out of sight, Rachel dashed
out to her car and took a change of clothes from her
trunk. She wasn't going to fire her first shot, as it
were, smelling of antiseptic and wearing clothes covered in who-knew-what. In the clinic's tiny bathroom
she stripped and took a soapy washcloth to all the
important places, touched up her makeup, put on the
clothes she'd brought, and fluffed out her hair. A
touch of cologne, and she was as ready as she was
ever going to be.

But it was too soon, of course. They would just
be sitting down to supper. So she pulled out the résumés and started reading. They were all promising.

After that, she took care of a dozen or more little
chores she hadn't had time to see to last week. Then
she took care of a few more that she wouldn't have
time to see to this week.

Finally, at seven, she saw Joe and Alma drive off
and head for home.

Now. It was time.

She wasn't expecting miracles, she reminded herself as she retrieved the cobbler from the refrigerator.
After all, Cody was there. But this was only her first
salvo. Well, her second if she counted Sunday in the
tack room.

After putting her dirty clothes and her medical bag
in her car, she drove down to the house and parked.

With her cobbler in hand, she dodged Harry's en-
thusiastic, three-legged greeting, took a deep breath,
and knocked on the front door.

Nobody answered.

It was inconceivable that she could have gone to this much trouble and then find out he wasn't at home. He had to be home. His pickup was here, and Joe and Alma had just left. She knocked again.

Finally the door opened.

She smiled brightly. "Hi. I brought—good grief! What happened to you?" His lip was swollen, his jaw was bruised, and one eye was turning a nasty shade of blue. He wore a steel-and-leather brace outside his jeans on his injured knee.

Behind him she heard a snicker of laughter. "He didn't eat his vegetables," Cody said.

Grady turned his head and looked down at Cody, slowly, it seemed to Rachel. As if it hurt to move.

"Smart mouth," he said.

Cody laughed and danced out of reach. "That's what you said when I asked."

Rachel raised a brow at Cody. "And did you eat your vegetables?"

"Sure did. See? Not a mark on me."

"And let that be a lesson to you," Grady said.

Rachel smirked. "I knew Alma was strict on you, but I had no idea."

"What can I do for you?" he asked. "As you can see, I'm not exactly up to entertaining."

"Or anything else," she muttered.

"What was that?" Grady asked.

Well, there was obviously no damage to his hearing. "Never mind. Cody, can you take this to the kitchen?" She held out the covered dish of cobbler.

"Sure. What is it?"

"It's a surprise. For later. No fair peeking. And be careful, it's heavy."

"Don't worry, Miss Dr. Rachel." He eyed his dad's bruises and grinned. "I'm minding *real* good today."

"For a change," Grady muttered.

"Aw, Dad."

"Aw, Cody."

Laughing, Cody headed for the kitchen, and Rachel dashed back to her car and retrieved her medical bag.

Grady eyed it as if it were a snake. "What's that for?"

"It's for you. Go sit down before you fall down. Do you need help?"

Slowly he turned and limped back to the living room as Rachel followed. He was hugging one arm to his chest as though his ribs hurt.

"You're too late," he said. "I've already been doctored up one side and down the other."

"At least you've got that knee braced. Now, while Cody's out of the room, what happened?"

"Wait," he said.

It must have been a parent's sixth sense. An instant later Cody dashed into the room.

"It's really not very funny," Cody said to Rachel while motioning toward his dad. "That ol' bull really stomped him a good one."

"That he did, pard," Grady said, easing himself down onto the recliner. "You wanna do me a favor?"

"Sure, Dad."

"Run out to the tack room and fetch that brown bottle of liniment. You know the one, don't you?"

"Sure, I know it. I'll be right back."

"I didn't mean—ah, hell. The kid runs every-where. Has since the day he learned how to walk."

"I'd love to hear about that," Rachel told him, "but right now I want to know what really happened to you. Tell me you did not get stomped by a bull."

He laid his head back and closed his eyes. "I got stomped by three of them."

"What?"

He opened his eyes and looked at her. "Sit down and promise me you'll let me have my say before you say or do anything."

Rachel was getting a really bad feeling about this. She sat on the chair next to his. "Okay, I promise."

"Promise me you won't try to do anything about this."

"About what? You don't want me to look at your injuries?"

"You can look till the cows come home. You can even doctor them if it makes you feel better—al-though I can do real fine without any more stitches, thank you very much. That's not what I'm talking about."

"What *are* you talking about?"

"Rachel, you have to be careful."

"Grady, I promise I'll be as gentle as possible."

"You're not listening," he said harshly. "I don't want you driving around this county by yourself. Do you hear me?"

That bad feeling she'd had a moment ago turned ugly. "Grady?"

"I went to town last night, and on the way home I got stopped."

Rachel's stomach clenched. "By Martin."

"You guessed it in one."

Her eyes widened. "Did he do this to you?" She came up out of her chair. "Did he?" she demanded.

"I'm not that easy a mark. He had help. He called out two of his deputies."

Rachel closed her eyes and held her breath. "Tell me one of them was not Dane Powell."

"No, Powell wasn't one of them."

"Thank God," she whispered. She would have died if she'd been that wrong about Dane. He was one of the good guys.

"They didn't need a fourth man. I can hold my own in a fight, but not against three walking refrigerators."

"Oh, Grady." She knelt beside his knees and looked up at his poor, battered face. "They hurt you."

"I'll be all right," he said. "But I admit I'm worried about you. After the way you told him off Saturday... I don't mean to scare you, Rach, but you be careful, you hear me? Don't give him any excuse to stop you. Don't let him catch you anywhere alone."

"I'll be careful, I promise."

"Do you still carry that varmint pistol in your car like you used to?"

She nodded. "Under the seat."

"Good. Make sure it's loaded. If Martin or one of his deputies tries to pull you over when you're out on a call, don't stop. You hear me, Rachel? Don't stop. You keep driving and drive straight into town, or somewhere else where you know there are people in plain sight."

"It's all right," she soothed. "Now that I'm warned, I'll be careful, don't worry."

"The smartest thing for you to do," he said in a

tight voice, "would be to stay as far away from me as you can get."

Rachel's heart skipped a beat. "Is that what you want me to do?"

"If it keeps you safe."

"That's not what I asked. But never mind," she said, determination building inside her. Sheriff Martin and his threats had forced Grady to leave five years ago to keep Cody safe. She would be damned if she let that man come between them again. "I'll decide what's smart for me and what isn't. How bad are you hurt?"

He laid his head back down and sighed. "Bad enough, but I'll live."

"Your ribs?"

"Just bruised and sore."

"How do you know? Did you go to the doctor this time?"

His lips twitched as he narrowed his eyes. "What do you think?"

She narrowed her eyes right back. "Who put in the sutures? And where are they?"

"Dr. Alma." He showed her the back of his left forearm. "She's had plenty of practice over the years."

Rachel studied the three sutures and found them clean and neat. She couldn't have done better. She wasn't sure she could have done it at all—sutured Grady's skin—without falling apart afterward.

She rested her forehead against the arm of his chair. "Oh, Grady, I'm so sorry."

Grady's chest tightened when he heard the tears in her voice. He couldn't stand that. "Hey." Placing a finger beneath her chin, he nudged her head up until she looked at him. Her deep blue eyes were swimming. "Don't, Rach. It's not your fault."

"I know, but—"

He placed his thumb over her lips to still them. "But nothing. He's hated me for five years. He's always going to hate me."

"What are you going to do? You can't let him get away with this. What will he do to you the next time he catches you out alone?"

"I'm going to be a hell of a lot more careful, for starters. And so are you. If a county sheriff's car tries to pull you over, you put that gun of yours in your lap and drive straight to town, like I said. Drive to the police station. You hear me?"

She nodded. "I hear you." She took his hand from her chin and kissed his bruised knuckles.

Grady felt that kiss clear down to his heels.

"I see you got in a few licks of your own."

He smiled wryly. "They didn't walk away clean. I'm sure they all had a little explaining to do when they got home." He looked down and for the first time noticed how Rachel was dressed. Kneeling below him as she was, her blouse dipped low and fell off one shoulder, showing skin so creamy-smooth-looking his fingers tingled with the craving to touch it. A little too much skin, if anyone were to ask him.

"Good God, woman. Tell me you didn't go on call dressed like that."

She fluttered a hand to her throat. "Why, this old thing?"

"Some lonely ol' rancher would have swallowed his tongue if you bared that much skin to him."

The smile that came across her mouth and lit her eyes was potent enough to scare him. She stood up slowly and placed one hand on each arm of his chair. Then she leaned down to him, her blouse gaping even more.

"I sure hope," she said in a sultry voice that made sweat pop out across his back and palms, "that you haven't swallowed yours."

The brush of her mouth against his was so gentle it was barely there, and yet he'd never felt a kiss more potent.

The front door slammed.

"I got it, Dad."

She pushed away and straightened slowly. "Nope," she said in that same siren voice. "It's still there. And I'm glad. I seem to remember you used to be rather...clever with it."

Grady blinked. Was she talking about his tongue? The tongue he was sure he'd just swallowed?

"Here it is, Dad." Cody bounded into the room with the bottle of liniment.

Grady had to clear his throat twice before he could speak. "Thanks, pard."

"You want me to rub that on for you?" Rachel said softly with a wicked gleam in her eye.

Yesterday she ran from him. Today, when he was in no shape to do anything about it, she was coming on to him.

"If I said yes," he told her, his eyes narrowed, "you'd run."

She laughed. "You wish."

"When do we get the surprise you brought?" Cody asked, setting the bottle of liniment on the table next to the recliner.

"Yeah," Grady said, relieved, maybe, to have the subject changed. "What'd you bring us?"

"Well," she said, drawing the word out. "Do you have room for a little dessert?"

"Oh, boy," Cody cried.

Rachel's hands shook all the way home that night. Whether it was nerves or excitement, she wasn't sure. But the look of shock on Grady's face when she'd kissed him did her heart good. She wondered if he knew his hands had trembled when he touched her just before she left.

She thought to stay away from him the next day, but decided against it. During a brief break in her schedule she stepped outside for some much-needed fresh air and walked down to the corral where Grady and Joe were doctoring some cuts on a yearling calf.

"You call a vet?" Grady asked Joe.

"Nope. Not me."

"Don't mind me," Rachel said. "I'm just stretching my legs." *You remember my legs, don't you, Grady? You used to like touching them, stroking them when I wore shorts or a skirt.*

He looked up just then and caught her gaze, and she sucked in a sharp breath. It was as if he'd heard her thoughts, the look in his eyes was so hot. Her heart raced. With a big smile, she turned and walked away. "See you later," she called back over her shoulder.

"What was that all about?" she heard Joe ask.

"Damned if I know," Grady muttered.

Later that afternoon, biting back a moan every time he moved, Grady remembered what had sent him to town the night before and put him in the path of Sheriff Gene Martin.

Toothpaste. "How's that for irony?" he muttered as he made his way to his pickup. A tube of toothpaste to keep his teeth clean had nearly got those same teeth knocked right down his throat. Toothpaste, a can of deodorant, shaving cream. A simple run to town for some basic personal needs.

By the time he'd made it home he'd forgotten about them. He opened the pickup door now to retrieve the sack and snarled at the dried blood staining the seat, the steering wheel, the floor mat. Little drops and smears all over the damn place.

"Well, hell." He grabbed the sack of items and took it into the house. There he filled a plastic pail with cold soapy water, then went back outside and tackled the cleanup. The steering wheel and the floor mat came clean with no problem, but the seat, covered in fabric rather than vinyl, was another matter.

Joe came over and stuck his head in the open passenger window. "Alma says, and I quote, 'tell him to get his rear in the house and get off his feet and that bad knee before he does more damage to himself.' Said she'd clean this up in the morning when she got back from grocery shopping."

Grady replied with a grunt. "I don't think even Alma can get this damn blood out." He threw his rag down in disgust. "Never did like these seats anyway. I still miss that custom-made fake-sheepskin seat cover I had in my old pickup. But then, if I'd got blood all over that, I'd have to kill Martin, and then I'd go to prison, and you'd have to raise Cody, and—"

"I get the picture. Anybody ever tell you you're about as friendly as a rabid skunk when you get your ego bruised?"

"My ego's just fine," Grady snarled. "I'm not ashamed of being bested by three hulking Neanderthals who outweigh me by about fifty pounds each."

"That's good to hear. Not that they outweigh you, but that your ego isn't as bruised as that pretty face of yours."

"What a pal." Dipping his fingers into the pail, Grady flicked soapy water at Joe's face.

"Hey!" Joe swiped a hand over his face. "You're never gonna get those stains out. Why don't you just get yourself another one of those custom seat covers you're so fond of?"

"I tried when I bought this rig, but the company I got the last one from is out of business. I never took the trouble to try and find another one."

"Well, while you're looking, why don't you see if the old one's still any good? It might come close to fitting."

"What old one? It's long gone by now, just like the pickup it was in."

Joe grunted. "Guess you haven't looked in the far shed since you've been back."

Grady frowned. "My old seat cover is in the shed?"

"I reckon it could be. Your old pickup is."

"You're kidding."

"Nope. Your dad always said some day you'd come home, and you'd want it when you did. He even kept up the tag and registration. The safety inspection would be long out of date, and who knows if it'll start after all this time, but it's there."

"I'll be damned."

The pickup was there, coated with enough dust to

choke an elephant, but it was there. And so was his custom-made, fake-sheepskin seat cover.

Memories by the dozen hit him in the chest at the sight of it. Memories of Rachel. Of all the times they'd snuck off to some secluded place after dark to make out, the way Rachel would sink her fingers into it and hold on while he pleasured her with his hands, his mouth. And then it would be his turn to hold on while she returned the favor.

Sometimes they would just talk, build their dreams, plan their future.

"Since the windows were rolled up, the inside's not so bad," Joe observed. "Considering it's been sitting out here for five years."

Grady took in as deep a breath as his bruised ribs would allow, and shook off the memories. He had enough trouble with Rachel in the present. No need to get himself all hot and bothered over their past.

"Now *that*," he told Joe, "is a seat cover."

He searched out the elastic straps that fit over the seat corners to hold the cover in place. The bottom corner on the passenger side, where Joe was helping, caught on something and wouldn't come free.

"I remember now," Grady said, circling the pickup. "There's a trick to it. Let me."

Joe stepped aside and Grady leaned in. He remembered that this side always hung on a spring underneath. He had to get his head right down on the floorboard so he could see what he was doing.

The cover came free, but so did something else.

"What the hell…" It was a small, hardbound book, with flowers on the cover, along with several dark stains that looked sickeningly familiar.

He had never in his life carried a book with flowers on the cover. Maybe it was some old book of Rachel's that had gotten accidentally kicked under the seat on their way home from college that last year, one of the last times he'd driven this rig. But he couldn't imagine her having a bloodstained book. He flipped open the cover, and felt like he'd been sucker punched.

This is the Personal and Private Diary of
LaVerne Marie Martin
Keep Out
Under Penalty of Death

Good God. LaVerne's diary? How the hell...

"Got it loose?" Joe asked from behind him.

"Uh, yeah." She must have had it with her the night he'd found her on the road and taken her to the hospital. The night Cody was born. The night she died.

He swallowed hard. The stains on the cover were blood. LaVerne's blood, from the beating her father had just given her.

"Well, get it on out of there and let's see if it fits."

"Uh, yeah. Right." But he wasn't ready to mention the diary to anyone just yet. Not until he got a good look at it.

He was going to feel like a heel reading through a dead girl's private diary, but he'd just have to get over it. The one thing Martin had hung over Grady's head, the one cold accusation he'd threatened to make that there would have been no way to disprove, could, maybe, be disproved in this diary. If LaVerne had written it down. This could be the lever he needed to force Martin to back off.

He bundled up the seat cover and slipped the diary into the folds. "I'll wash it first."

Rachel spent the rest of that week and all of the next putting herself in Grady's path every chance she got. Never for very long, and never when there might be an opportunity for genuine privacy. Not that there ever was such an opportunity, what with Louise and Jimmy and Alma and Joe and Cody around all the time.

But that was all right for now. She wasn't ready to go that final, irrevocable distance yet. He didn't want her enough, wasn't eager enough yet. She wanted to tease them both with anticipation. She wanted him as desperate for her as she was for him.

And, she wanted to work up her nerve. It was one thing to tease and lure, quite another to deliver the goods, so to speak.

Then, too, she wanted to see that look of wariness fade from his eyes.

Grady was just about ready to bite nails—and not the kind that grew on fingers. The kind a man pounded into wood with a heavy hammer. He didn't know what Rachel was up to, but he knew he couldn't take much more.

Not that he didn't like it, this...whatever it was she thought she was doing. The teasing, the sexy clothes. The way she kissed him, then danced out of his reach, leaving him panting and ready to beg.

It could all only mean one thing—that she really did want him. Unless she'd decided on this particular torment to get back at him for what she thought he'd done five years ago, but he couldn't believe Rachel was that calculating.

He'd been the one to hesitate and pull back that day in the tack room. She had offered herself to him, and that had been genuine. And what had he done? He'd questioned her, made her think he didn't want her. When she'd fled the barn that day, he'd thought that was the end of it. That she'd taken his hesitation as rejection. And he'd decided that was for the best.

Now here she was, day after day, reeling him in like a fish on the line. And he was flopping around at her feet, ready to beg for mercy.

But there had been no chance for privacy. There was always someone around when she came twitching that tight little rear his way, leaving her perfume on the air. On his clothes. His hands.

She was doing it on purpose, that much was clear. Making sure they were never alone.

Tonight would be different. It was Friday, and he'd given Alma and Joe the weekend off. At noon he had met Belinda in town and she had taken Cody to spend two nights at the Flying Ace. Rachel would bring him home when she went out there for supper Sunday afternoon.

Tonight, there was no one here but him.

If she didn't show up, he'd probably have to cut his own throat.

Someone knocked on the door.

He gave himself a final look in the mirror. Clean, pressed shirt, pressed jeans, and his boots were shined. His hair was combed, and he'd just shaved. His hands were clean. His bruises had finally faded a couple of days ago, so at least he was his normal color again. He was as ready as he would ever be.

No amount of preparation on his part could have readied him for the sight that greeted him when he opened the door.

She'd worn a dress. Except for the day of the funeral, he hadn't seen her in a dress since college. And he'd never seen her in a dress like this. It was red, what there was of it. Some kind of stretchy knit thing that looked like it had been spray-painted on. A tube top, nothing more, that covered her from the swell of her breasts down to the tops of her thighs and not an inch more. It was a come-on dress if he'd ever seen one, and he was more than ready to oblige.

Her legs went on for a mile, clear down to a pair of flimsy red sandals with spike heels.

"Hell-o-o. My face is up here."

Grady swallowed. Hard. "If you wanted me to look at your face, you shouldn't have worn that excuse for a dress." But finally his gaze trailed up that mile of legs and that little bit of red, over bare swells, and up to her face. Her eyes looked different. Not their color, but their expression. Mysterious. Dangerous. Her hair was all curls. He'd never seen curls in her hair before.

She raised her arms out from her sides and turned in a circle. "You like?"

His hands started to tremble. He swallowed again, looking her up and down. "That sound you just heard was me swallowing my tongue."

"Well, now." She sidled up to him and slipped her arms around his neck.

Her perfume made him think of sex. As if he needed any help.

"That's a crying shame," she told him, pulling his face down toward hers. "Let me see." She pressed her lips to his and dipped her tongue between them. "Ah, good," she murmured, then stroked his tongue with hers. "There it is."

Grady clamped his hands on her and performed his own search of her mouth. The kiss left him panting for more. He flexed his fingers on her bare shoulders.

"Are you going to invite me in?"

That sultry, come-hither tone in her voice sent hot tingles dancing down his spine. "Are you sure you want to come in? There's no one here but me. No buffers tonight, Rachel. No Cody to give you the excuse to tease and run."

Her smile was downright dangerous. "Who do you think suggested this was the time for his sleep-over with my nephews?"

"Planned it all, did you?"

"They wanted to invite him. I just suggested the timing, that's all."

"Why?" he asked bluntly.

"Why do you think? Do I have to spell it out for you?"

"Yes. You have to spell it out."

She stepped back, propped her hands on her hips—which made the hemline of that red thing creep up enough to have him sweating—and cocked one hip. "Because I've decided you're going to be my first lover, and I was hoping that by now you'd be over this hang-up you seem to have about my virginity."

While he stood there wondering if maybe he really had swallowed his tongue this time, she leaned down and hefted a red leather bag that he hadn't noticed. That he hadn't noticed a bag big enough that, if she were boarding a plane, they'd make her check it, well, that was understandable under the circumstances, he figured.

"Now," she said, hoisting the bag to her shoulder. "Are you going to invite me in or do I have to stand here and beg?"

She sounded like she was more inclined to argue than beg, but far be it from him to deny the woman when she had her mind made up. Although her behavior tonight and all the teasing she'd thrown at him during the past couple of weeks was a side of Rachel he'd never seen before.

She'd never been a pushover, but she'd never been aggressive with him this way, either. He wasn't quite sure how to react. He knew what he wanted to do. He wanted to haul her over his shoulder and tumble her straight into bed, where he would peel her out of that red thing like she was a banana. Then he would gobble her up.

But just two weeks ago, he remembered as he stepped aside and ushered her into the house, he had essentially pushed her away. Why was it he'd done that? Oh, yeah. Virginity—hers. Terror—his. And the truth. The truth he needed to tell her but hadn't. The truth he now had the means to prove.

He could tell her right now, and he should. But she seemed to have genuinely put the past behind her. How much sweeter that she would take him on faith that he wouldn't betray her again, by giving herself to him before she learned he'd never betrayed her at all.

But how unfair of him to keep something that important from her. And there were other things she should be considering before they took this irreversible step.

She tossed her bag onto the sofa and spun toward him. "I'm thirsty."

He'd just bet she was. Probably scared spitless over what she was about to do. She couldn't have changed so much that the idea of making love for the first time wouldn't make her at least a little nervous. But then, they'd done everything *but* that final act more times than he could count back when they were young and hot for each other. She'd never been a bit shy then.

"No beer," she said quickly, holding her hand up palm out.

"Not if you begged," he told her. "How about a soft drink?"

"Yes. Please."

While he was out of the room, Rachel pressed a hand to her stomach and ordered herself to calm down. She was getting to him, she could tell. If tonight went as she hoped, she would be taking the biggest step of her life, and she was ready for it. Wanted it. With him. She didn't want to lose a single second of it to nerves.

She closed her eyes and took three deep breaths. When she opened them again, he was there, watching her, a sweating glass of iced soft drink in each hand.

"That didn't take long," she said inanely.

He crossed the room and handed one of the glasses to her. Took a drink from his. "You're nervous."

"I guess I am, a little."

"You should be." He took another drink, obviously not planning on helping her through this. "This could be the biggest mistake of your life."

She sipped, stalling, then said, "I'm aware of that."

"Are you? A lot of people around here still remember the way I left town so fast."

"And?"

"They still talk about it. They'll talk about you, if you get paired up with me again. You don't want—"

"Don't tell me what I want."

"And there's the sheriff to consider."

"He's not here right now, so he's not a consideration. Why are you trying to talk me out of this?" The ice in her glass rattled because her hands were shaking. She set the glass on the coffee table. "I'm not asking for promises. I'm not trying to stake a claim on you or pick up where we left off years ago. I'm not even asking you not to betray me again."

"Rachel—"

"I'm only asking for whatever you're willing to give me. If all you can give me is tonight, so be it. If you don't want me, Grady, just say so."

"Not want you?" He set his glass next to hers and moved closer. With the tips of his callused fingers, he traced a path from her wrists to her shoulders, then back down again. "There hasn't been a day of my life that I haven't wanted you since I was old enough to know what it meant."

Her knees threatened to give way. She reached out to him for support. "Then why are we standing here talking?"

Chapter Eleven

He carried her to his bedroom. With every step he took her words echoed in his mind. She wasn't looking for promises or claims. But he wanted to make promises. He wanted to stake claims. They should never have been separated. She was the other half of his soul. He'd been a fool to try to live without her. If she could forgive and forget his imagined wrong, then he could put aside her part in causing their separation.

The sun was still up, but the blinds were closed, filling the room with soft, muted light. Just inside the door he stopped with her in his arms and jammed one heel into the bootjack, kicked off that boot, then did the other.

She was correct. It was all in the past, and there was no place for it here. This was right. As he stood her next to his bed, he knew that what they were about to do was right.

"Wait," she breathed when he pulled her close. "I forgot. In my bag."

But he was tired of waiting. He'd waited a lifetime for this, and she'd spent the last two weeks deliberately stirring him up. He pressed his lips to her bare shoulder and tasted her with his tongue.

"Condoms," she said on a gasp. "In my bag."

"Condoms." He kissed his way up her neck, then leaned over and opened his nightstand. "In my drawer."

"Shouldn't we..." Her tongue flicked out and moistened her lips. "Open one?"

"In a minute." But first he had to taste where her tongue had just stroked. It was as sweet as he remembered, but she was trembling. He pulled back and looked into her deep blue eyes. "Scared? Or nervous?"

"Nervous, I guess."

"We don't have to do this, Rachel. Not if you're not sure."

She closed her eyes and took a deep breath.

Grady prayed for her to be sure. Prayed for that strip of red to stay in place, strained though it was as her chest expanded.

"I'm sure. It's just the waiting is killing me."

"It's killing me, too." He smiled slowly. "It's supposed to."

She returned his smile. "Okay. Let's make it worse." She reached for the buttons on his shirt and started undoing them.

Fair enough, he thought, since once he peeled that dress off her, he was going to be a goner.

With his shirt unbuttoned, she spread her hands across his chest, then leaned into him and rubbed her cheek against him. The feeling was so exquisite, he moaned.

"You're harder than you used to be."

He closed his eyes and nudged his hips against hers. "I know."

She chuckled. "I meant your chest. Oh, how I've missed your chest." She pushed his shirt off his shoulders and down his arms to let it fall to the floor. "Your arms are harder, too. I like you this way."

He slid his hands across her back and discovered that the taunting red fabric moved with them. Her body had changed, too. She was fuller, more rounded than he remembered. A woman now rather than a girl. "I like you this way, too."

He took her mouth with his and peeled her dress down to her waist. His hands slipped unerringly to her breasts. "I like you this way even better."

Rachel closed her eyes in wonder as, for the first time in five years, a man's hands gave her pleasure. This man's hands. The only man. "Grady...oh, Grady, I've missed you."

He took her down to the bed and it seemed the most natural thing in the world to feel him settle his weight between her thighs.

"And I've missed you," he told her, raising himself up on one elbow to look at her.

She thought she would be shy, feel awkward, when he looked at her. No man had seen her naked since...since he had. But the desire in his eyes took away any shyness she might have felt. Instead, she felt pleased and proud that the sight of her put that much hunger in those blue-green eyes.

"I've missed touching you." He smoothed a hand up her ribs to cup one breast, to tease her nipple with his thumb.

Rachel arched into his touch, silently begging for more.

"I've missed tasting you." He bent and flicked her nipple with his tongue.

She nearly came off the bed, so powerful was the sensation that shot through her. How could she have forgotten? Had it ever been this powerful before, this hot? Had she ever felt so needy? She was on the verge of flying apart. How was she ever to withstand his full assault?

Then he took her nipple into his mouth and she cried out at the sheer pleasure. Everything inside her shifted, tightened.

Grady felt her response, saw it in the flush on her cheeks. Urgency built in him. He forced himself to go slow, when his body urged him to plunge. To take. To make her his once and for all time.

He teased them both by trailing his mouth to her other breast, tasting it, sucking it, treasuring it. Then he kissed his way down the center of her chest until he reached the bunched fabric of her dress. Greedy now for the rest of her, he moved to her side and pulled the dress all the way off, and with it, the narrow strip of red lace beneath.

"Beautiful," he murmured. "So beautiful."

But he wasn't touching her, and she couldn't stand it. She wanted his weight on her, his hands. His mouth. His skin. She wanted his skin. With a whimper of protest, she reached for his belt buckle with hands that trembled. "Help me."

Her whispered plea sent heat and blood pooling in

his loins. Together they stripped him of the rest of his clothes, and her hands were suddenly everywhere. Everywhere but where he wanted them most. And then they were there, stroking him, grasping him, strangling the breath in his lungs.

"No more," he begged. He sounded helpless, he knew. And he was. Helpless against wanting her, needing her. Helpless against the sensations, the emotions she brought to life inside of him.

Condom. Mustn't forget. He reached for one, tore open the packet, and felt her gaze as if it were her hands while he put it on. Then he was there, cradled in the welcoming warmth of her thighs.

Slow. Easy. He had to be both or he would hurt her. He would rather die than hurt her. This was her first, he was her first. The very thought humbled him.

He reached between their bodies and stroked her, drank her moan of pleasure with his mouth. With his hand, he pleasured her the way he used to do on hot summer nights in his pickup, when they had done everything to and with and for each other except the actual joining of their flesh.

"Remember how it used to be?" he whispered.

"Was it this good?" she managed.

"It couldn't have been. We'd have died of it. Let go, Rach. Look at me and let go, the way you used to."

"Grady…"

He could feel the tension vibrate inside her and echo in his loins. He stroked her again, and her eyes went blank, her neck arched. She cried out.

Now. Now he would take her, while the pleasure still rode her. He cupped her face in both hands and kissed her, deep and hard as he positioned himself and slowly, to cause her the least discomfort possible, eased his way inside. It was the hardest thing he'd ever done as he fought the need to plunge.

But it was worth it. She was worth anything.

With small, gentle nudges, he pushed his way inside, rocking, kissing, whispering words of encouragement. She closed around him like a tight, velvet fist, hot and wet, searing him with her heat, pulling him in deeper, deeper, until he felt the barrier.

"Hold on to me, Rach," he whispered. "Hold on to me."

Rachel wrapped her arms around his back, her legs around his waist. She felt him there, where no man had ever been. There was discomfort in the stretching, but there was more—a sense of fullness, of overwhelming emotion that made her eyes sting. He rocked against her, and she rocked back. Then there was a slight tearing sensation that had her sucking in a sharp breath.

"I'm sorry," he whispered. "I'm sorry. That's the worst of it, I promise."

"Shh." She soothed him with her voice, with her hands in his hair. "I'm fine. It's…I feel you," she said in wonder. "I feel you inside me. Oh, Grady, it's…"

"I know." And he did. He'd had other women, but this was a first for him, too. For he was joined, flesh inside flesh, with the only woman he'd ever loved. He was, for the first time in his life, fully and completely home.

Gradually he felt her relax, and then she moved beneath him, and his waiting was over. The flames licked at him, and he welcomed them, let them have their way. Higher, harder, hotter, and Rachel was with him every inch of the way. He felt the pressure of her nails on his back and savored it. He felt her slick heat, her racing heart, her labored breath, and they matched his.

And then he felt her tense, her inner muscles grip him as she found her release. With one final thrust, he let go and joined her.

Before she'd even caught her breath, Rachel knew she'd only been fooling herself. She wasn't willing to accept whatever he might be willing to give her. She wanted it all. She wanted to make love with him like this every night for the rest of her life. She was utterly, completely in love with him. She had told herself that she had survived his betrayal once, she could survive it again if she had to, but she'd been wrong. Holding him close in her arms and feeling his labored breathing, she knew that if he hurt her again, she would die.

He stirred in her arms. Oh, it was heaven holding him this way, feeling his skin against her skin, his flesh still inside her, his weight anchoring her solidly to him. If only they could stay this close....

Grady levered himself onto his forearms and looked down into blue eyes swimming with emotion. There were so many things he wanted to say to her, promises he wanted to make, promises he wanted to hear from her lips. But the words lodged in his throat, and the only thing that came out was, "Are you all right?"

She sniffed and nodded, her smile wobbly but brilliant. "I've never been more all right in my life."

Slowly he eased out of her, not wanting to add to whatever soreness she was bound to feel. He rolled over and pulled her onto his chest. "Stay with me," he said. "Stay the night with me, Rach." *Stay forever.* But he couldn't say it. Not yet, not until he told her the truth. "Stay the weekend."

Rachel's heart swelled. It was a start. It was more than she'd hoped for. "I have to work tomorrow."

"So do I, but come here after. Alma and Joe are gone for the weekend, and Cody—well, you know about that," he said, smiling, "since you're bringing him home Sunday. But he's never spent the night away before. I might get scared if I have to stay here all by myself."

"Don't worry." She snuggled closer. "I'll protect you."

"I knew I could count on you." Then he kissed her to seal the bargain.

"Come with me Sunday," she said. "To the ranch."

He looked at her from the corner of his eye. "Will there be a lynching?"

She laughed. "I doubt it. You'll be welcome there."

Finally he nodded. "Okay."

They made love again, then Grady gave her an all-new experience in the shower. Afterward they rifled through Ray and David's video collection and found a copy of *High Noon*. With a bowl of popcorn balanced on Grady's washboard stomach, they slid the cassette into the VCR and ate popcorn in bed while quoting all the best lines to each other.

Grady knew that he could never let her out of his life again. She had to love him. She couldn't have given herself to him if she didn't love him. Could she?

But any discussion of a future between them was likely to become tense, because he fully intended to force her to listen to him this time as he finally told her the truth about LaVerne and Cody.

So that discussion would wait, because this night belonged to the magic of simply being with her.

The next morning, after reluctantly watching her walk up to the clinic for the day, he spent hours planning what to say to her, how to bring the subject up. But by the time she came back to him Saturday evening, he had missed her so damn much that it took three long, deep kisses to steady him.

Then he backed away and held her at arm's length.

Rachel saw the serious expression in his eyes and felt her stomach tighten. Here it comes, she thought. He was going to tell her...what? That he didn't want her anymore? She couldn't believe that. Not after the way he'd just kissed her.

"What?" she finally asked him when he just stood there and looked at her.

He took a deep breath before speaking. "You said you didn't want any promises."

The nerves in her stomach wound tighter. "Yes. I did."

"That's not good enough for me. I do want promises. If that's going to be a problem for you, tell me now, Rach."

Her pulse began to race. Nothing ventured, nothing gained. She gulped in a breath and said, "I've changed my mind about that. I want promises, and more."

"More?"

"I love you, Grady."

"Rachel…"

"If you feel the same way, I want us to get married."

Grady thought his knees might fold up any minute. "You trust me that much, when you haven't ever let me tell you—"

"We weren't married back then. If we get married now, I'll expect you to stay faithful until the day you die. Last night I said I could survive if you betrayed me again, but I was wrong. I couldn't, Grady. I just couldn't."

"I would never, ever, betray you with another woman."

"Again."

"What?"

"You would never betray me again. I want you to say it, Grady." She'd thought about nothing but this all day long. More than once since moving back home he'd said he wanted to tell her the truth about what happened. She didn't want to hear any details. It would kill her to hear him talk about sharing with LaVerne Martin what he'd shared with her last night. It nearly killed her just to think of it.

But sometimes she got the impression that he thought *she*, Rachel, had somehow wronged *him*, by not listening to him that day he'd come to see her.

"I don't want any details, please," she told him. "But if you would just admit that you cheated on me and promise never to do it again, we'll call it done. I want you to admit it once, and then I don't ever want to talk about it again."

His hands slid from her shoulders and he stepped

back. "That's mighty generous of you," he said tightly.

"I'm not trying to be generous. I just want us to clear the air, that's all."

"Oh, we'll clear the air, all right. You wouldn't listen to me five years ago, but by God, you're going to listen to me now. If you love me the way you say you do, you owe me that much."

"*I* owe you?"

"That's right."

Oh, God. Why had she opened her mouth? She'd been much happier with her head in the sand. She should never have asked him to admit it. Now he was angry, and she was getting that way herself, and everything was ruined.

"You all but pushed me out of your house and slammed the door in my face that day. One phone call, one lousy phone call from some damn nurse you went to school with, and you believed every word she said without ever once asking me if it was true."

"I—"

"You never asked, Rachel. You never said, 'Grady, tell me it isn't true.' All you said was get out. Well, I got out, but no more, dammit. This time you're going to listen if I have to hog-tie you."

Anger drained out through her toes and left a sick feeling in its wake. "I don't think I can take this." She turned away, unable to bear hearing him talk about his having slept with LaVerne.

"I think you can, Rachel."

"No." With panic chasing her, she ran for the front door.

"Rachel, dammit, I'm not Cody's father."

She stopped, whirled. "You would lie? Now? After last night, you would stand there and lie to me? Oh, God!''

She made it to her car and spewed gravel all the way to the highway. Never. She could never trust him again. To lie about such a thing... He might as well have reached inside her chest and ripped out her heart with his bare hands.

It felt like she was dying.

Grady stood in shock as she ran out of the house. Damn her. She hadn't believed him. She claimed she loved him, yet she refused to trust him enough to listen. She wouldn't listen five years ago, and she wouldn't listen now.

The hell she wouldn't. She wasn't getting away with it this time. With determined strides, he went to the safe in his father's office and retrieved the diary. If Rachel wouldn't believe him, maybe she'd believe LaVerne.

He almost caught up with her on the highway, but not quite. He considered it a good sign that the sheriff wasn't around to catch him speeding. He wasn't in the mood to go another round with three goons. Although the way he was feeling just then, he figured he could have taken them all on and come out on top this time.

''Damn her.''

When he hit the edge of town he saw her three blocks ahead as she turned off Main onto the street where she lived. By the time he pulled up behind her in her driveway she was slamming her front door shut. He grabbed the diary, marched up her steps, and pounded on her door.

With each blow of his fist to her door, Rachel flinched. "Go away!"

"I'm not going away. Open the door."

His voice rang with fury. What did *he* have to be angry about, damn him? Just because she didn't want to listen to more lies? Or worse, the truth about how he'd slept with LaVerne? A shudder worked its way down her spine at the thought of listening to that particular tale.

No way. She wasn't going to listen, he couldn't make her listen.

At least the pounding had stopped. Maybe he'd given up and gone away. She wanted him to. She was sure of it.

She went to the front window and tried to see out the crack in her drapes. His pickup was still there behind her car, but—

"You really should learn to lock your back door, Rach. No telling who might walk in—"

She whirled on him. "Uninvited," she finished for him. "All right, you're in. Say what you have to say, then get out."

"Oh, yeah," he said, half under his breath. "She really loves me, all right."

"I'll get over it." She saw him flinch. "Go ahead," she said. "Spill your guts about how you ended up in bed with that little—" She stopped and took a deep breath. She would not speak ill of a dead girl who couldn't defend herself. She would not speak ill of the mother of a little boy she adored.

"No," Grady said slowly. "I don't think I am going to tell you what really happened. You've already made up your mind not to believe me, haven't you?"

"If you're going to tell another whopper about not being Cody's father, when he's the spitting image of you, I'm not likely to believe a word you say. How can you deny that sweet little boy? What kind of man are you? How could I ever have thought I loved you?"

"I can't imagine, but when you figure it out, let me know. Meanwhile, since you won't believe me, maybe you'll believe this."

She eyed the book he held out to her as if it were a particularly poisonous snake. "What is it?"

"It's pretty interesting reading, actually. It's LaVerne's diary." He tossed the journal onto her sofa and pulled open the front door. "And just for the record, there's a reason Cody's eyes are brown, like David's."

He couldn't have shocked her more if he'd suddenly grown elk horns on his head. "Grady?"

He stopped with his hand on the door knob and looked over his shoulder. "Have I finally got your attention?"

"Grady, what are you saying?"

"Read the diary, Rachel."

"You're...you're leaving?"

"I'm going home." He closed the door quietly behind him.

Rachel stood in the center of her living room for a long time and shook.

August 10

Dear Diary:
She doesn't deserve him. She's not woman enough for a man like Grady Lewis. But I am.

They're leaving for college in a few days. I don't have much time to get him to notice me.

August 14

Dear Diary:

I can't believe what I did tonight. Celebrated my eighteenth birthday in grand style. Grady leaves for Laramie tomorrow, so I hung out at the Wagon Wheel. I told Daddy I was meeting girlfriends there. I don't think he believed me, but he didn't say anything. As of today, I'm an adult, so what could he say?

Anyway, I went to the Wagon Wheel because I heard Grady and she—her?—no, she would be there, with their families. A going-away party to send them off together. I got him out on the dance floor once—had to drag the sorry so-and-so. But then Rachel came along and took him away. She's always taking him away.

But I showed him. Or at least, that's what I set out to do when I found his brother at the church wiener roast in the park. It was easy to lure him away. He's not too smart. Before tonight I would have called him a dumb retard. Have, as a matter of fact, several times. All I had to do was tell him Grady was waiting for him, and he came right along like a trained puppy on a leash.

I figured, if I can't have Grady, David will do. If he knew how to do it, that is. Ha ha. I was desperate, or I never would have bothered with David. But I have to be able to throw it in

Daddy's face that I made it with an Indian. He hates Indians, ever since Mama ran off with that Cherokee from Oklahoma when I was ten. The mean ol' goat's been taking it out on me ever since, and I'm tired of it. So tonight, I showed him.

I'm not sorry, either. I figured I might be, seeing as how it was David I was making it with instead of Grady. But you know what? David was so sweet, and he got so excited that I laughed, but he didn't care. He laughed too. He didn't make fun of me or call me names like some of the boys I've done it with have.

Maybe I won't tell Daddy. In fact, I better not, or he'll take out after David when he's through hitting me, and poor David is too sweet and innocent to protect himself from a bully like my daddy.

I guess it's a good thing Grady's leaving town in the morning, though, because when Grady found David on my porch and drove off with him, Daddy pulled up and saw him leave. But he only saw Grady. So I guess I got what I wanted. Daddy knows I made it with an Indian. He's just guessing the wrong Indian.

Rachel trembled as she continued reading. In her own hand LaVerne told of finding out she was pregnant, of knowing it was David's child she carried. When her father found out about her condition, she'd kept David's identity a secret. Her father knew she ran fast and loose, so when he accused her of not knowing who the father was, LaVerne let him think that was true. Then he'd remembered seeing Grady drive away from their house that night, and assumed he was the father. And she let him think that, too.

Then she told of her father shipping her off to her aunt's in Casper so no one in Wyatt County would know she was pregnant. He told her she could come home whenever she wanted, but not with a baby. It was up to her if she got rid of the baby now, or after it was born. Either way, he wanted nothing to do with it. He had his position in the county to think of. He didn't want people thinking he couldn't even control his own daughter.

Rachel had never held any affection for LaVerne Martin, but the entries she wrote in her diary while at her aunt's stirred her to pity. The girl had been achingly homesick. She'd missed her friends, and had even missed her father.

But if Sheriff Martin was stubborn, his daughter was more so. She'd decided she wanted to have her baby at home in Hope Springs, and she was going to keep it. She would love it and raise it, and it would love her. Finally, somebody would love her.

LaVerne hadn't thought there would be anything wrong with the baby, like there was with David. She knew that David hadn't been born retarded. He'd gotten that way by getting kicked in the head by a horse when he was little.

Her last entry was from the night before she planned to leave for home.

Rachel closed the diary and ran her hand over the cover. It was stained. Just like LaVerne's life. Like her death.

A drop of water dripped onto the back of Rachel's

hand and rolled off onto the book's cover. A tear, she thought in dull surprise.

She knew what had happened, or most of it, after LaVerne had come home. She must have returned the same evening Rachel and Grady came back from Laramie that year. Grady had taken Rachel to the Flying Ace, then had headed home. She remembered that it had been nearly midnight when he dropped her off.

He would have had to drive back through town to get to the Standing Elk. He'd told them at the hospital that he'd found LaVerne wandering beside the road, beaten and bloodied.

Had she had the diary with her? Was that how Grady ended up with it?

LaVerne had given birth that night to a baby boy who looked a great deal like the man who'd brought her to the hospital. She'd given Grady's name for the blank on the birth certificate marked "father."

Then the sheriff had arrived, and LaVerne had died. Of childbirth complications compounded by internal injuries from the beating she'd received. The sheriff had blamed Grady and said that he was turning the baby over to the state to be put up for adoption.

From Dr. Ray she'd learned that he and Grady had tried to stop the sheriff from taking the baby. After all, Grady was listed as the father. But when they went to see the district judge, the sheriff—the judge's cousin, no less—came swaggering out of the judge's chambers with a possum-eating smile on his face.

As the baby's father, Grady was a single, unmarried college student with no job. The baby's grandfather was a highly respected county sheriff, who felt the baby would be better off being adopted by a family that would be able to give it every advantage. That was what the judge told them.

Grady hadn't stood a chance. He had done the only thing he knew to do to protect the baby. He'd taken him and run.

But not before trying to explain to her, Rachel thought.

And she hadn't listened. Hadn't let him explain. Hadn't trusted him enough, hadn't believed in him.

"God, Grady. I'm so sorry." If only she had listened to him, believed in him. They could have been married, and with his father and her brothers helping them, they could have provided a home for Cody that no judge would have quarreled with, not even Sheriff Martin's cousin. Grady wouldn't have had to leave everything and everyone he'd ever known to keep his brother's son from being raised by strangers.

Realizing the magnitude of what she had caused, Rachel put her head down on LaVerne's diary and wept. She wept for herself, for Grady, for Cody, for Dr. Ray. And oh, God, she wept for David. She even wept for LaVerne. But mostly she wept for Grady, for it was he who paid the highest price for her lack of faith.

With one hand braced beside the patio door, Grady nursed a beer and stared out into the backyard and the lengthening shadows.

Was she reading the diary? Would she believe it? She had to. God, she had to.

Had he been too hard on her, too angry? Too mean?

He pressed his forehead against the glass door and

closed his eyes, willing her to come. She had to come.

"You really should learn to lock your front door. No telling who might come in—"

"Invited," he said, whirling toward her, his heart thundering, his mouth suddenly dry. "Always invited."

"Even—" She stopped, steadied herself "Even after the way I've acted?"

"You read it?"

She nodded. A tear slipped down her cheek, and the sight of it nearly killed him.

She looked everywhere but at him. "I...I don't know how you can stand the sight of me."

He shrugged and gave her a sad smile. "I love you. I've always loved you."

"After the way I treated you?"

"I won't say it didn't hurt when you turned me away and wouldn't listen to me, but there's enough blame to go around. It's eaten at me for years that I could have found a way to make you listen."

She smiled sadly and finally looked at him. "The way I was feeling then, I doubt that." She closed her eyes. "But when I think that if I'd listened, maybe you wouldn't have had to leave, I get sick to my stomach."

"I still would have had to leave," he said.

"Not if we'd have gotten married and provided Cody with a stable home. No court would have taken him away with your father and my brothers behind us."

"Maybe not, but the sheriff would have claimed David forced himself on LaVerne and had him locked away in an institution for the rest of his life. I couldn't chance that.''

Rachel's eyes widened. ''The sheriff knew about David? How?''

''LaVerne. Apparently she threw it in his face the night she came back from Casper, and that's what prompted the beating he gave her.'' He closed his eyes and tilted his head back. ''He said if he ever found the baby within a hundred miles of this county, he'd parade a dozen girls into court who would claim David had forced himself on them, too.''

''Oh, my God. Did your father know?''

''No.'' Grady swallowed. ''I couldn't tell him. For as far back as I can remember, he blamed himself for David's accident. He would have blamed himself for this, too, for not preventing it somehow. He wouldn't have let me leave. He certainly wouldn't have helped me the way he did, giving me his car and dipping into his savings so I'd have enough to get by on until I settled somewhere. He never expected me to be gone for so long. He thought he could talk sense into Martin.'' Grady shook his head. ''Maybe I should have told him the truth.''

''No,'' Rachel said. ''No, Grady, don't do that to yourself. It would have killed your father to stand by and watch one son sacrifice everything he'd ever known in order to save the other. And he would have hurt so bad for David, that he would never know he had a son.''

''But David did know.''

''What? How? Did you tell him? Did he understand?''

Grady shook his head again. ''I didn't tell him. I didn't think he would understand. The first time he and Dad came out to see me, Cody had just turned one. Remember how David was? Sometimes he remembered every word a person told him. Sometimes he remembered for a while, then forgot.''

''And sometimes he didn't remember at all,'' she said with a poignant smile. ''But he never forgot a person.''

''No, never. He might not have remembered how or why he knew them, but he knew the face and name of every person he'd ever met.''

''And he remembered LaVerne?''

Grady cleared his throat. ''Uh, yeah.''

Rachel nearly smiled. ''And?''

''And…he also remembered the birds-and-bees talk Dad had given him. His thoughts might have been those of an eight-year-old, but his body belonged to a grown man. He knew what sex was, and that it made babies. He knew he'd…how was it he put it? He said he'd 'done the dirty' with LaVerne.''

''Your father wouldn't have taught him that sex was dirty.''

Grady bit back a grin at her outrage. ''I asked David about that, about why he called it that. He said he heard it on TV. Anyway, he took me outside one day when they were visiting and told me all of this and told me he thought maybe he'd given LaVerne her baby. That he'd given her Cody.''

Rachel put a hand to her mouth and blinked rapidly. ''What did you do?''

''I asked him if he'd told anybody. He said no, so I told him not to. He said—'' Grady had to stop and let the sudden lump in his throat subside. ''He said he knew he couldn't take care of a baby, so it was good that I was doing it, and that he didn't want Dad to know, because he'd promised Dad that if he ever thought he wanted to have sex, he would talk to him first. He didn't want Dad to be disappointed in him.''

"Oh, God.'' Another tear slipped from beneath her closed lids and streaked down her cheek. "Oh, poor David. Your father would never have been disappointed in him.''

"No, but it would have been one more thing for Dad to feel responsible for. He would have decided it was his fault. He would have tried to make me bring Cody home.''

"How could he? What choice would he have had against the sheriff's threats but to keep Cody away or risk David's freedom?''

"None,'' Grady said bluntly. "In the end, none.''

"Wait—what about the diary? Why couldn't you have used that to prove David hadn't forced himself on LaVerne?''

He shook his head again. "I didn't know it existed until last week.''

"What?''

He told her about finding it in his old pickup out in the shed.

Then Rachel asked, "Why did you stay away so long, Grady? Why didn't you bring Cody and come home? Surely after a while...''

"Dad thought it would be best, and I agreed with him, that I shouldn't bring Cody back here as long as Gene Martin held any position of authority in this county. For the last election Dad said he did his damnedest to get somebody to run against Martin, but nobody was willing. Then last winter he said he'd found the perfect person, an outsider, to run in the upcoming election this fall. He never said who it was, though.''

''But…after all these years. You had the birth certificate. Wouldn't that be enough to keep the sheriff from taking Cody away?''

''Not if he'd pushed for a DNA test. He could have proved I wasn't Cody's father.''

''What about now? Couldn't he still do something now?''

''No.'' Grady shook his head. ''I made damn sure of that years ago. I hired myself a fancy California lawyer, and I legally adopted Cody. Gene Martin can't touch him.''

''Yet you still didn't come home?'' she asked, distress etching new lines on her face. ''Why, Grady?''

Evading her gaze, Grady looked out the door beside him at the deepening dusk.

''Grady?''

He shrugged. He had vowed to tell her the truth, and this was part of it. But he didn't want to hurt her again. ''The longer I stayed away, the easier it got. It wasn't as if I could just pick up my old life right where I'd left it.''

Another tear rolled down her face. ''And the girl you trusted to believe in you had sent you away. Oh, God, Grady.''

''Don't, Rachel. I made my own decisions. I'm not saying they were all smart ones, but they were all mine.''

They stood there and looked at each other for a long time as darkness settled outside the glass door and seeped into the room. And they hurt. And wanted. And yearned.

''You're still the only woman I've ever loved,''

he told her quietly, his voice rough with emotion. "The only woman I will ever love."

"How can you," she cried helplessly, "after what I've done?"

"How can you love me after thinking all these years that I betrayed you?"

Rachel was nearly choking on a combination of anguish and hope. "I didn't know. I didn't know I still loved you until you came home, and I saw you again, and I just...couldn't help myself."

Humbled beyond belief, and grateful that her heart was strong enough to forgive what she thought he'd done, Grady crossed the six feet of empty floor that separated them. "Marry me, Rachel Wilder. Be my wife. Be Cody's mother. Make more babies with me. I swear to you, I will spend the rest of my life making sure you never have to doubt me again."

Rachel's eyes filled with tears. "Marry me, Grady Lewis. Be my husband. Let me be Cody's mother. Make more babies with me. Forgive me and marry me and I swear, I will spend the rest of my life loving you, believing in you, and never doubting you again."

They came together with hearts too full for words.

Epilogue

A pile of giggling little boys and a grinning dog the size of a small sofa greeted Rachel and Grady in the yard when they pulled up at the Flying Ace the next day.

Rachel had talked Grady into coming with her. He still wasn't convinced his reception would be painless. Her brothers were going to take one look at her face and know how she'd spent the last two nights and most of this morning. There was a look in her eyes that threatened to melt his bones every time he saw it. No way could her brothers miss it.

"Dad!" Cody called. "Look, guys, it's my dad!"

"Hey, pard. Looks like you're having a good time."

"Ah, naw, we're just doing boring stuff." Cody then spoiled his nonchalant reply by bursting into giggles.

"Yeah," Grady said. "I can see that."

"Oh, good." Belinda poked her head out the back door. "You're here. We're just about ready to sit down. Come on in."

"You go on," he told Rachel.

"Grady, you can't stay out here like a coward. It's a roast they're carving up in there, not you."

"I'll be along in a minute," he said. "I want to talk to Cody first."

"Oh." Rachel hadn't been a bit nervous about telling her family she and Grady were getting married. But thinking what Cody's reaction might be to suddenly learning he was going to have to share his father with another person had her breaking out in a cold sweat. "All right. I'll just…go on in."

Grady snagged Cody and held him back while the other boys trooped into the house with Rachel.

"Aren't we gonna go eat with everybody else?" Cody asked.

"In a minute." He squatted next to the child of his heart, so he could meet him at eye level. "I've got something I want to ask you."

Curious, Cody cocked his head. "Sure, Dad. Is something wrong? Do we gotta move back to California?"

"No. It's nothing like that. We're not ever moving back, Cody. This is our home now. I thought you liked it here."

"I do! I don't wanna live nowhere else, Dad. This is the best place in the whole world."

Grady smiled and ruffled the boy's hair. "I think so, too. And I think, if you're willing, it's about to get even better."

"Huh?"

* * *

"Where's Grady?" Belinda asked when Rachel entered the kitchen and joined the rest of the family.

"He's coming," she said, her gaze darting around the room.

Ace stopped behind his chair and pierced her with a narrow-eyed, all-seeing gaze. "What's wrong?"

If her smile was a little on the tense side, it was the best she could do. "Nothing." What if Cody didn't want a mother?

"Then why do you look like a Thanksgiving turkey waiting for the axe to fall?"

"Gee, thanks." She stuck her tongue out at him.

Her nephews giggled.

"Oh, I don't know," Jack said. "I think she looks more like the Road Runner when it looks down and realizes the ground is gone."

The three youngsters giggled again.

"The Road Runner," Jason said, snorting.

Clay hooted. "That's a good one, Uncle Jack."

"You are too cute for words, all of you." Rachel yanked her chair out and sat down.

"Leave the girl alone," Trey said, eyeing her closely.

The back door opened and closed as Grady and Cody came in, saving Rachel from any more brotherly comments. She looked up anxiously, but could read nothing on Grady or Cody's face. They were holding hands. Was that a good sign? Or bad?

"There you are," Belinda said. "Grady, the seat next to Rachel's is yours. Cody, you know where your seat is."

"Thanks." Grady nodded, but stood where he was, holding on to Cody's hand.

The room fell silent as everyone wondered why they were just standing there.

"It's going around," Ace muttered. To Grady he said, "Is anything wrong?"

"No. At least, not yet," he added with a wry smile.

"What's that supposed to mean?" Ace asked.

Grady glanced around the table, sizing up what he hoped would not turn out to be the enemy. "Ace," he said with a nod. "Jack, Trey, Belinda, boys. Cody and I have talked it over, and we'd like your permission—no, that's not right." He shook his head. "It's going to happen anyway. But we'd like your blessing. Rachel and I are going to get married."

Even the refrigerator quit humming, as if it didn't dare break the sudden, stunned silence in the room.

Slowly, Jack grinned. "Well, it's about damned time."

Trey smirked at Rachel. "Guess he got over that shyness, and you got over your—hey, why'd you kick me?"

Ace ignored that and eyed Grady sharply. "I take it you two have already talked this over?"

"We have," Grady said with a decisive nod.

"Rachel?" Ace asked.

"Ace," she said between teeth that were clenched tight.

"Oh, my word."

All eyes turned to Belinda as she stared at Grady, a huge smile covering her face.

"I just remembered where I've seen you before."

"What are you talking about?" Ace asked irritably.

"When I saw Grady when he first came back, the

day of the funeral, I thought he looked familiar, but I couldn't place him.''

''Can this wait?'' Ace asked. ''We're in the middle of something kind of important here.''

Belinda shot her husband a look. ''No, it can't wait. You're just hedging anyway. You know you're going to give in. But it might make you feel better if you hear that where I saw him before was in Fort Collins at Rachel's graduation in May.''

If Rachel's heart had been racing before, now it threatened to swell right out of her chest. ''You were there?''

He gave her a half smile. ''I knew how much you wanted it. I couldn't help it. I had to see you graduate.''

''Oh,'' she cried, her eyes filling. She leaped from her chair and dashed around the table, throwing herself into his arms and covering his face with kisses. ''Oh, Grady.''

Suddenly Ace smiled, then laughed. ''I don't know if it's a blessing or a curse, but it's yours. Welcome to the family, you two.''

* * * * *

*For the next book
In Janis Reams Hudson's
compelling saga*

WILDERS OF WYATT COUNTY,

here's a preview of

A CHILD ON THE WAY,

*available only from
Silhouette Special Edition in
September 2000.*

Jack Wilder scrunched his neck down inside the turned-up collar of his sheepskin coat and cursed the weather forecasters for predicting nothing more than a light dusting of snow. He cursed the mountains for not trapping the storm on the western slope and keeping it there. He cursed himself for not heading down out of the back country yesterday when he ran out of coffee.

Light dusting, be damned. It wasn't merely snowing now. What they had here was their first full-fledged, gen-u-ine blizzard of the season. The wind cut through thin clothing and bare skin like a hot knife through butter. The good news, Jack thought with grim humor, was that even if the wind did slice him to ribbons, it would be impossible for him to bleed to death—it was too damn cold for blood to flow.

Skeezer tossed his head and snorted. The fool horse actually enjoyed weather like this.

Visibility decreased by the minute. Jack knew he'd be worse than a fool to try to make it all the way home in this weather, when he could stop at the vacant section house. Skeezer would be out of the storm in the barn, and Jack could build a fire in the living-room fireplace; never mind that there wouldn't be any furniture or electricity.

Jack urged Skeezer over the crest of the final hill and down the other side where the wind wasn't quite as sharp. The land spread out before him covered in a smooth blanket of white. Acre after acre, mile after mile, even if he couldn't see much of it for the blowing snow. He knew it was there. Flying Ace land. Wilder land. Home.

A thick stand of cottonwood and willows bordered the creek at the base of the hill. Skeezer waded into the creek, not minding the freezing water, and out the other side. When they broke through the trees, Jack knew the building that normally housed the foreman for the southwest section of the ranch was less than a mile ahead.

Away from the shelter of the hill, the wind sliced with renewed vigor. They trudged on, man and horse, heads down. Jack's fingers, toes and face were going numb by the time the section house appeared before them out of the blowing snow. The house was white, so it was hard to see, but it was there.

If the car had been white, Jack might not have noticed it where it rested nose-down in the ditch next to the driveway. He hadn't expected to see a car. There shouldn't have been one on this road at all, let alone in the ditch. If the car hadn't been red and only partially covered with snow, he might have missed it. Some traveler had really gotten lost. Jack just hoped no one was hurt.

He drew Skeezer to a halt beside the car and swung down from the saddle. With his forearm he brushed the snow off the driver's side window and peered in. His stomach dropped.

The driver was a woman, with a face as pale as the snow. She sat slumped over with her head against the steering wheel, her ashen face turned toward him, her eyes closed.

She was unconscious.

Jack rapped on the window. "Ma'am? Lady, can you hear me?"

No response.

He opened the door and felt warm air against his face. She hadn't been here too long, then, or the interior of the car would have been as cold as the air outside.

How badly was she hurt?

Who was she, and what the hell was she doing out here? Nobody could get to this place by accident. She would have had to have turned off the highway and driven under the big Flying Ace sign at the ranch entrance, and then right through headquarters and past the big house. After that it was nothing but miles of rangeland.

Puzzled and concerned, he called to her again while pulling off his gloves. When he got no response he reached for her shoulder. God, she looked delicate. Felt delicate beneath his hand, even through her heavy coat. "Ma'am? Come on, honey, wake up."

Still no response.

She seemed to be breathing all right, and when he checked her pulse, it felt normal. Not too fast, not too slow; not thready or weak.

But she was so damned pale. So damned still.

He needed to get her out of this cold, yet he was reluctant to move her until he knew how badly she was injured. From the tire tracks still just visible in the snow, she couldn't have been going very fast. She must have hit her brakes and skidded sideways before landing nose-down in the ditch. The snow already piled up in the ditch would have cushioned the impact. The worst she probably had was a bump on her forehead where she'd hit the steering wheel, and a busted radiator.

Reaching into the car, he checked her arms and legs for broken bones, then carefully felt her neck.

She moaned once, shifted her head.

The movement of her head reassured him that her neck wasn't broken. That had been his main concern, and even that hadn't seemed likely.

She moaned again, and her face scrunched up in a frown.

Snow White, he thought, taking in her unnaturally pale face. And again the word *delicate* came to mind. And *beautiful*. Her skin looked as soft and smooth as white satin. For a minute he was tempted to stroke one creamy cheek to find out. Or kiss those pale lips…

Bad idea. The woman was unconscious. She wasn't Snow White, and he damn sure wasn't anybody's Prince Charming. Maybe when she came to…

Jack lowered his gaze. His eyes nearly bugged out of his head. She was pregnant!

You have just read a

Silhouette

Special Edition

book.

Silhouette Special Edition always features incredible authors like Nora Roberts, Sherryl Woods, Christine Rimmer, Lindsay McKenna, Joan Elliott Pickart—and many more!

For compelling romances packed with emotion always choose Silhouette Special Edition.

Silhouette®
™ *Where love comes alive*™

Now that you have enjoyed a
special edition
why not try some more?

On sale July 2000:

The Pint-Sized Secret
Sherryl Woods

Jeb Delacourt was supposed to find out who was selling the family firm's secrets—not fall for the prime suspect! Did Brianna O'Ryan have something precious to hide?

Man of Passion
Lindsay McKenna

Loner Rafe Antonio reluctantly agreed to protect beautiful Ari Worthington while she ventured through the Brazilian jungle. Could Rafe keep his own heart safe from the woman he'd sworn to keep from harm?

Married to a Stranger
Allison Leigh

Jaded tycoon Tristan Clay knew that a marriage of convenience was the only way to help Hope Leoni. But Hope was already in love with her groom—and now Tristan had to admit his heart wasn't as resistant as he'd thought!

**Each month there are six new
Silhouette Special Edition books to choose from.**

Silhouette®
Where love comes alive™

If you enjoyed what you just read,
then we've got an offer you can't resist!

Take 2 bestselling
love stories FREE!
Plus get a FREE surprise gift!

Multi-*New York Times* bestselling author

Nora Roberts

knew from the first how to capture readers' hearts.
Celebrate the 20th Anniversary of Silhouette Books
with this special 2-in-1 edition containing her fabulous
first book and the sensational sequel.

Coming in June

Irish Hearts

Adelia Cunnane's fiery temper sets proud, powerful horse
breeder Travis Grant's heart aflame and he resolves to
make this wild ***Irish Thoroughbred*** his own.

Erin McKinnon accepts wealthy Burke Logan's loveless
proposal, but can this ravishing ***Irish Rose*** win her
hard-hearted husband's love?

Also available in June from
Silhouette Special Edition (SSE #1328)

Irish Rebel

In this brand-new sequel to ***Irish Thoroughbred***, Travis and
Adelia's innocent but strong-willed daughter Keeley discovers
love in the arms of a charming Irish rogue with a talent for
horses...and romance.

Where love comes alive™

where love comes alive—online...

your romantic
life

➤ Talk to Dr. Romance, find a romantic recipe, or send a virtual hint to the love of your life. You'll find great articles and advice on romantic issues that are close to your heart.

your romantic
books

➤ Visit our *Author's Alcove* and try your hand in the Writing Round Robin—contribute a chapter to an online book in the making

➤ Enter the *Reading Room* for an interactive novel —help determine the fate of a story being created now by one of your favorite authors.

➤ Drop into *Books & More!* for the latest releases—read an excerpt, write a review and find this month's Silhouette top sellers.

your romantic
escapes

➤ Escape into romantic movies at *Reel Love,* learn what the stars have in store for you with *Lovescopes,* treat yourself to our *Indulgences Guides* and get away to the latest romantic hot spots in *Romantic Travel.*

All this and more available at
www.eHarlequin.com
on Women.com Networks

ATTENTION
LINDSAY McKENNA FANS!

Coming in April 2000 from Silhouette Books:

This special 3-in-1 volume contains the
three exhilarating novels that began the popular
MORGAN'S MERCENARIES series!

Coming in July 2000 from Silhouette Special Edition:
MAN OF PASSION

Coming in August 2000 from Silhouette Books:
MORGAN'S MERCENARIES:
HEART OF THE WARRIOR

A brand-new, longer-length book!

Only from Lindsay McKenna and
Silhouette Books.

SILHOUETTE'S 20ᵗʰ ANNIVERSARY CONTEST
OFFICIAL RULES
NO PURCHASE NECESSARY TO ENTER

1. To enter, follow directions published in the offer to which you are responding. Contest begins 1/1/00 and ends on 8/24/00 (the "Promotion Period"). Method of entry may vary. Mailed entries must be postmarked by 8/24/00, and received by 8/31/00.

2. During the Promotion Period, the Contest may be presented via the Internet. Entry via the Internet may be restricted to residents of certain geographic areas that are disclosed on the Web site. To enter via the Internet, if you are a resident of a geographic area in which Internet entry is permissible, follow the directions displayed on-line, including typing your essay of 100 words or fewer telling us "Where In The World Your Love Will Come Alive." On-line entries must be received by 11:59 p.m. Eastern Standard time on 8/24/00. Limit one e-mail entry per person, household and e-mail address per day, per presentation. If you are a resident of a geographic area in which entry via the Internet is permissible, you may, in lieu of submitting an entry on-line, enter by mail, by hand-printing your name, address, telephone number and contest number/name on an 8"x 11" plain piece of paper and telling us in 100 words or fewer "Where In The World Your Love Will Come Alive," and mailing via first-class mail to: Silhouette 20ᵗʰ Anniversary Contest, (in the U.S.) P.O. Box 9069, Buffalo, NY 14269-9069; (In Canada) P.O. Box 637, Fort Erie, Ontario, Canada L2A 5X3. Limit one 8"x 11" mailed entry per person, household and e-mail address per day. On-line and/or 8"x 11" mailed entries received from persons residing in geographic areas in which Internet entry is not permissible will be disqualified. No liability is assumed for lost, late, incomplete, inaccurate, nondelivered or misdirected mail, or misdirected e-mail, for technical, hardware or software failures of any kind, lost or unavailable network connection, or failed, incomplete, garbled or delayed computer transmission or any human error which may occur in the receipt or processing of the entries in the contest.

3. Essays will be judged by a panel of members of the Silhouette editorial and marketing staff based on the following criteria:

   > Sincerity (believability, credibility)—50%
   > Originality (freshness, creativity)—30%
   > Aptness (appropriateness to contest ideas)—20%

   Purchase or acceptance of a product offer does not improve your chances of winning. In the event of a tie, duplicate prizes will be awarded.

4. All entries become the property of Harlequin Enterprises Ltd., and will not be returned. Winner will be determined no later than 10/31/00 and will be notified by mail. Grand Prize winner will be required to sign and return Affidavit of Eligibility within 15 days of receipt of notification. Noncompliance within the time period may result in disqualification and an alternative winner may be selected. All municipal, provincial, federal, state and local laws and regulations apply. Contest open only to residents of the U.S. and Canada who are 18 years of age or older, and is void wherever prohibited by law. Internet entry is restricted solely to residents of those geographical areas in which Internet entry is permissible. Employees of Torstar Corp., their affiliates, agents and members of their immediate families are not eligible. Taxes on the prizes are the sole responsibility of winners. Entry and acceptance of any prize offered constitutes permission to use winner's name, photograph or other likeness for the purposes of advertising, trade and promotion on behalf of Torstar Corp. without further compensation to the winner, unless prohibited by law. Torstar Corp and D.L. Blair, Inc., their parents, affiliates and subsidiaries, are not responsible for errors in printing or electronic presentation of contest or entries. In the event of printing or other errors which may result in unintended prize values or duplication of prizes, all affected contest materials or entries shall be null and void. If for any reason the Internet portion of the contest is not capable of running as planned, including infection by computer virus, bugs, tampering, unauthorized intervention, fraud, technical failures, or any other causes beyond the control of Torstar Corp. which corrupt or affect the administration, secrecy, fairness, integrity or proper conduct of the contest, Torstar Corp. reserves the right, at its sole discretion, to disqualify any individual who tampers with the entry process and to cancel, terminate, modify or suspend the contest or the Internet portion thereof. In the event of a dispute regarding an on-line entry, the entry will be deemed submitted by the authorized holder of the e-mail account submitted at the time of entry. Authorized account holder is defined as the natural person who is assigned to an e-mail address by an Internet access provider, on-line service provider or other organization that is responsible for arranging e-mail address for the domain associated with the submitted e-mail address.

5. Prizes: Grand Prize—a $10,000 vacation to anywhere in the world. Travelers (at least one must be 18 years of age or older) or parent or guardian if one traveler is a minor, must sign and return a Release of Liability prior to departure. Travel must be completed by December 31, 2001, and is subject to space and accommodations availability. Two hundred (200) Second Prizes—a two-book limited edition autographed collector set from one of the Silhouette Anniversary authors: Nora Roberts, Diana Palmer, Linda Howard or Annette Broadrick (value $10.00 each set). All prizes are valued in U.S. dollars.

6. For a list of winners (available after 10/31/00), send a self-addressed, stamped envelope to: Harlequin Silhouette 20ᵗʰ Anniversary Winners, P.O. Box 4200, Blair, NE 68009-4200.

Contest sponsored by Torstar Corp., P.O. Box 9042, Buffalo, NY 14269-9042.

ENTER FOR A CHANCE TO WIN*

Silhouette's 20th Anniversary Contest

Tell Us Where in the World You Would Like *Your* Love To Come Alive... And We'll Send the Lucky Winner There!

Silhouette wants to take you wherever your happy ending can come true.

Here's how to enter: Tell us, in 100 words or less, where you want to go to make your love come alive!

In addition to the grand prize, there will be 200 runner-up prizes, collector's-edition book sets autographed by one of the Silhouette anniversary authors: **Nora Roberts, Diana Palmer, Linda Howard** or **Annette Broadrick**.

DON'T MISS YOUR CHANCE TO WIN! ENTER NOW! No Purchase Necessary

Silhouette®
Where love comes alive™

Visit Silhouette at www.eHarlequin.com to enter, starting this summer.

Name: _____

Address: _____

City: _____ State/Province: _____

Zip/Postal Code: _____

Mail to Harlequin Books: **In the U.S.**: P.O. Box 9069, Buffalo, NY 14269-9069; **In Canada**: P.O. Box 637, Fort Erie, Ontario, L4A 5X3

*No purchase necessary—for contest details send a self-addressed stamped envelope to: Silhouette's 20th Anniversary Contest, P.O. Box 9069, Buffalo, NY, 14269-9069 (include contest name on self-addressed envelope). Residents of Washington and Vermont may omit postage. Open to Cdn. (excluding Quebec) and U.S. residents who are 18 or over. Void where prohibited. Contest ends August 31, 2000.   PS20CON_R2